MONTANA MAVERICKS

Welcome to Big Sky Country, home of the Montana Mavericks! Where free-spirited men and women discover love on the range...

BROTHERS AND BRONCOS

Romance is in the air for the ranchers of Bronco, but someone is watching from the sidelines. A man from the town's past could be behind the mysterious messages, but does he pose a threat to Bronco's future? With their happily-ever-afters at stake, the bighearted cowboys will do what it takes to protect their beloved town— and the women they can't live without!

SUMMER NIGHTS WITH THE MAVERICK

Most gals would find sweet-talking charmer Wes Abernathy irresistible, but single mom Everlee Roberts is trying her darnedest not to. Her cowboy may be a prince but he's also a player, and he's too young to think of settling down. When the sun goes down, however, she can feel her resistance to Wes weakening...

Dear Reader,

Sometimes love finds us when we're not even looking for it. Love can show up to complicate and enrich our lives just when we've decided that giving our hearts is simply too risky or too difficult. When we've promised ourselves we're not going there again.

Everlee Roberts and Weston Abernathy have both been thoroughly disappointed in love. Everlee, a hardworking single mom, doesn't even have time for romance right now. She might be willing to give her heart again later, when her little daughter is older, after she's made her career dreams come true. But certainly not now.

And when Everlee does say yes to love again, it definitely won't be with the hot and charming Weston. Yes, the wealthy rancher is tall, lean and tempting. But Wes is only out for a good time—and Evy has no room for any of that.

As for Wes, he gave his heart once and got it back in pieces. Never again. Now he likes his relationships casual and fun—and Evy's a woman a man needs to take seriously. He knows he should leave her alone. Yet he's captivated by everything about her. He can't stop thinking of her and can't stop showing up at Doug's bar, where she works, hoping that one of these nights she'll give him a chance.

Yep. The road to true love is often unpaved and full of potholes. Wes is not ready for that. Neither is Evy. Still, I'm betting on love to win out. And I'm guessing that you are, too...

Happy reading everyone,

Christine Rimmer

Summer Nights
with the Maverick

CHRISTINE RIMMER

Special thanks and acknowledgment are given to
Christine Rimmer for her contribution to
the Montana Mavericks: Brothers & Broncos miniseries.

HARLEQUIN®

**SPECIAL
EDITION™**

PLEASE RECYCLE

THIS PRODUCT IS RECYCLABLE

Recycling programs
for this product may
not exist in your area.

ISBN-13: 978-1-335-72401-4

Summer Nights with the Maverick

Copyright © 2022 by Harlequin Enterprises ULC

Harlequin Enterprises ULC
22 Adelaide St. West, 41st Floor
Toronto, Ontario M5H 4E3, Canada
www.Harlequin.com

Printed in U.S.A.

Christine Rimmer came to her profession the long way around. She tried everything from acting to teaching to telephone sales. Now she's finally found work that suits her perfectly. She insists she never had a problem keeping a job—she was merely gaining "life experience" for her future as a novelist. Christine lives with her family in Oregon. Visit her at christinerimmer.com.

Books by Christine Rimmer

Harlequin Special Edition

Wild Rose Sisters

The Father of Her Sons
First Comes Baby...

The Bravos of Valentine Bay

Almost a Bravo
Same Time, Next Christmas
Switched at Birth
A Husband She Couldn't Forget
The Right Reason to Marry
Their Secret Summer Family
Home for the Baby's Sake
A Temporary Christmas Arrangement
The Last One Home

Montana Mavericks: Six Brides for Six Brothers

Her Favorite Maverick

Visit the Author Profile page
at Harlequin.com for more titles.

A thousand thanks to Amy Tapia and Carmen Julie Mall. Together, Amy and Carmen named the sweet rescue kitten in this story. At their suggestion, the kitten became Valentina, for the heart-shaped marking at the base of her tail. Amy and Carmen, this one's for you.

Chapter One

Everlee Roberts wished she had wings on her ugly black anti-slip working shoes.

At eight in the evening on July 2, Doug's bar in Bronco, Montana, was packed and likely to get more so. From the regular folks right there in Bronco Valley to the rich ranchers and other power brokers who lived in Bronco Heights, the whole town loved to hang out at Doug's. It was that kind of place, the kind where everyone was welcome, and no one sat alone.

On a night like tonight, the jukebox played non-stop, a cowboy could wait hours for his turn at a pool table and anyone who wanted to be heard above the din would just have to shout. All the scarred wooden tables were full.

As for the bar, forget finding a seat. Every stool had an occupant—except the famous haunted stool, of course. According to local legend, if you sat on that stool, you were just looking for trouble. Folks claimed that a guy named Henry Jamison with a talent for playing the stock market once sat on that stool. Henry promptly lost everything in a deal gone bad.

And Henry wasn't the only one to lose big after daring to claim that stool. A happily married fellow went home to find the wife he adored in bed with another man. It got worse. Not that long ago, one unfortunate customer named Bobby Stone even died after taking a seat on that stool—or so the legend went.

For years now, Doug Moore, the bar's owner, had kept that stool roped off with yellow caution tape. Recently, Doug had taken things a step further. He'd added a sign that warned: Death Seat. And even on a night like tonight, when Everlee couldn't serve the drinks fast enough and customers constantly jockeyed for a chair, no one took a chance on the haunted stool—so far, anyway.

But never say never.

After all, it was day one of Bronco's four-day

Independence Day celebration, Red, White and Bronco. People were ready to party. And that meant that someone might yet end up braving the threat of that stool.

Just that afternoon, the Miss Bronco Beauty Pageant had taken place in Bronco Park. The winner? Charity John, a local rancher's daughter. After two years as first runner-up, Charity had finally claimed the crown. Just about everyone in town had rooted for the pretty blonde. She was smart, beautiful, kind and talented. The perfect Miss Bronco.

As for Everlee, a Miss Bronco contender herself a while back, tonight she was raking in the tips. She zipped around between the tables and the bar, racing to fill orders swiftly. Fast service, after all, meant even better tips.

Working the floor at Doug's was not Everlee's dream career. But it brought in a lot more than checking groceries or cleaning house for the rich folks in Bronco Heights. True, now and then a random cowboy might get a bit grabby, but she knew how to put most of them in their place with a warning look—and if things somehow slipped out of her control, Doug would step in and deal with the problem. Doug Moore might be well into his eighties, but he knew how to handle a badly behaved cowpuncher.

"Everlee!" shouted a baby-faced cowboy. "'Nother round, pretty lady!"

She pointed at her nametag and cheerfully shouted right back. "What'd I tell you, handsome? Call me Evy!"

The cowboy put on a pouty face. "Aw, c'mon, beautiful. Doug calls you Everlee. Why can't I?"

"Because you're not Doug!" The smooth, commanding voice came from over by the door. A shiver of unwilling awareness ran down Evy's spine. Weston Abernathy had arrived, his four hot and handsome brothers in tow.

Abernathy was an important name in Bronco. Weston and his brothers were cattlemen who had it all—including the endless, rolling acres of their beautiful ranch, the Flying A.

Not that Evy cared in the least that Weston was hot and rich. A hardworking single mom with an amazing little girl to raise, she had no spare time and zero energy to waste obsessing over some guy. Ignoring the fluttery sensation in her belly, Evy sent Wes a quick nod of acknowledgment and kept on moving.

Because when it came to good-looking, charming rich men?

Uh-uh. Never again. Been there. Saw the movie. Bought the T-shirt—and came away sadder and a whole lot wiser.

The Abernathy brothers immediately snagged the only empty table in the place. They reached it just as the family who'd been sitting there for a couple of hours conveniently decided it was time to head home. Evy dropped off a trayful of drinks at a corner table and served the baby-faced cowboy his pitcher of beer. She delivered two heaping platters of Doug's famous chili cheese nachos to an eight-top by the dance floor.

After that, she went on over to wait on the Abernathy boys—including Wes, who really was way too good-looking. Not to mention fun and friendly with a great sense of humor and dazzling sea-blue eyes.

Sam, the busman, cleared the table.

Evy quickly wiped it clean. "Okay, what can I get for you boys?" She gave Sam his damp towel back and off he went with a full tub of dirty dishes.

The brothers ordered a couple of pitchers along with some nachos, sliders and fries. She gave them all her brightest smile and said she'd be right back with the beer.

In the split second before she made her escape, Wes asked, "How're you doing, Evy?" Such a simple, innocent question. Nothing charged or meaningful about it. Just one of those things people say when they're making small talk.

And yet that question had her stomach swooshing and her mind going dead blank. "Uh. Great, Wes. Just great."

He looked at her so steadily. "That's what I wanted to hear." And then he smiled that crooked smile of his, the one that made her wish for things that were never going to happen.

"Great," she said—again. Because apparently *great* was her new favorite word. "Well, I'll be right back with that beer." And off she went, her cheeks too warm and her heart beating far too fast.

As she took another order and then made a quick stop at the bar to pick up the two pitchers, she reminded herself that she was twenty-five years old, a grown woman. She needed *not* to fumble for words like a smitten preteen every time Wes Abernathy said hello.

The mental talking-to helped. She managed to serve the Abernathys their drinks and then their food without stumbling all over herself.

True, now and then as the evening progressed, she caught herself glancing Weston's way and loving that delicious little thrill that vibrated through her every time her eyes met his. Each time that happened, she sternly reminded herself to cut it out right now.

But why did he always seem to be looking right at her when her gaze strayed in his direction?

They'd been doing this for months now, kind of dancing around each other.

Way back last summer, the first time she'd waited on him, he'd asked her where she'd been all his life. She had granted him a cool smile. "Busy. Very busy. What'll you have?"

That had shut him up. But not for long.

The next time he came in, he tried again. She'd set his beer in front of him and he'd asked her what she was doing Friday night.

She came back with, "Working. And I never go out with customers."

"Well, Evy, I'm really hoping I can find a way to change your mind about that."

She just shook her head and moved on to the next table full of thirsty cowboys.

For several months after that, until well past Christmas, he came in less often and when he did, he never seemed more than mildly friendly. She'd wondered if he'd met someone—and then she'd reminded herself that it was *good* if he had a special someone now. A special someone meant he was done flirting with her.

Now and then, though, even during those months when he seemed to be keeping his distance from her, she would feel his gaze on her, warm and intense. She just knew he was about to make a move on her again.

But he didn't.

For a while, she'd been certain she'd discouraged him permanently—which was good, she'd reminded herself. She didn't *want* him pursuing her.

But then lately, he'd started showing up more often. And every time she glanced his way, those blue eyes were waiting. He hadn't tried to ask her out again or anything. But she got that feeling that he wanted to, that he was working up to it. She had a sense that he was biding his time, waiting for an opening, that any night now, he would try to strike up a real conversation with her, try to find a way to get closer to her.

Now she really had her guard up with him. Whenever he spoke to her, she would answer as briefly as possible—and race off to wait on someone else.

So far, she'd never exchanged more than a few words with him per encounter. She had every intention of keeping it that way, too, though she found it more and more difficult to resist the invitation in those fine eyes of his. She had to constantly remind herself not to go there with him, to concentrate on doing her job, to keep things strictly professional. She took special care never to stand in one place long enough that he might make a real move, might try to get her to meet him for coffee, or even ask her out.

At least tonight, staying on the move presented no challenge at all. Doug's only got busier as the hour got later. It seemed like everyone in town was hanging out at the bar tonight—including ninety-five-year-old Winona Cobbs, Bronco's resident psychic.

Slim and delicate looking, almost birdlike, Winona was one of a kind. Not only was she smart and eerily perceptive, but she had her own distinctive style. Evy loved a woman with style. Someday, she hoped to open her own little shop where she could help the women of Bronco express themselves through bright, unique, reasonably priced fashion.

Tonight Winona wore a gold-spangled white Western shirt with a sequined pink vest and pink jeans. Her tooled white boots gleamed with gold thread and rhinestones. A pink turban crowned with a bobbing white feather covered her snow-white hair.

Evy admired Winona's great outfit, and then, for no reason at all, turned to look at Weston. He saw her do it and gave her a grin.

What was the matter with her? The whole point was *not* to go ogling Wes. Evy straightened her shoulders and swiveled her head back around—to find Winona staring right at her.

The network of wrinkles deepened on the old woman's narrow face as she slowly smiled. She actually winked at Evy and crooked a finger, beckoning.

Resigned, Evy went to her.

"Love in bloom," Winona said sweetly. "Such a beautiful thing."

People said Winona was not only psychic, but that she also had a knack for putting couples together. Folks in town claimed Winona paired people up and set them on the road to true love.

Well, Evy wanted none of that ridiculousness. "Sorry," she said to the psychic. "You've got it all wrong. Love is not on the menu, at least not for me." Before the old woman could come back with some mysterious pronouncement about taking a chance on romance, Evy turned the tables on her. "But tell me all about *your* love life, Winona."

The white feather on her turban bobbed as Winona laughed. "My love life? Well, I will say this much. When it comes to love, it's never too late…"

"You need to knock that off," muttered Garrett, Weston's oldest brother.

"No idea what you're talking about." Wes took a gulp of his beer.

Garrett grunted. "You're always staring at her."

Wes, like their younger brother Crosby, was a lighthearted guy as a rule, but he could level an icy stare with the best of them. He turned a freezing look on Garrett. "Staring at who?"

Garrett scoffed. "So that's how you're going to play it."

"Drink up." Wes indicated his brother's full mug. "Relax for once."

Garrett shook his head—but he did shut up about Evy.

Over at one of the pool tables, their brother Dean had just beat Tyler, the youngest of the five of them. Dean gave Garrett the high sign.

Garrett nodded at Dean and said to Wes, "My turn at the pool table." He shoved back his chair. "We all right?"

"Always," Wes replied.

Garrett clapped Wes on the shoulder and left to grab a cue.

Wes sat back and surveyed the action.

On the dance floor, his brother Crosby was two-stepping with a pretty blonde in a yellow dress. The blonde seemed fun and flirty—and Crosby laughed at something she said.

Wes's gaze strayed to Evy again. She was passing out food orders two tables over, smiling so pretty, nodding as one of her customers asked her a question.

Okay, fine. Garrett had a point. Wes shouldn't be staring at Evy. He shouldn't be thinking of her

all the time. Shouldn't be constantly trying to figure out how to get close to her.

But he was.

He wanted to start a real conversation with
her, wanted to move beyond, *Hi, how are you?*
He wanted to take her out, get to know her, spend
a little quality time with her.

He had that feeling about her—that she really
did like him. A lot. He just knew she felt as powerfully attracted to him as he did to her. And yet,
she avoided him at every turn.

The first time he'd spotted her, almost a year
ago now, right here at Doug's, he'd thought, *That
girl, right there. I want to get closer to her...*

Damn, she was pretty, with shining black hair
and eyes green as shamrocks.

From the first, he'd admired the proud way she
carried herself, enjoyed the musical sound of her
laughter. Men tried to cozy up to her. She never
gave any of them more than good service and a
friendly smile. It was no different for him. The
first time he tried to talk to her, she'd shut him
right down.

He began asking around about her and he'd
learned that she had a daughter named Lola. Folks
said that Evy had met some guy in college, but
it hadn't worked out. She'd moved back home to
Bronco to have her baby.

Once he'd learned about little Lola—who was four now from what he'd heard—Wes had decided to leave Evy alone.

He liked his interactions with women to be easy and casual. It felt wrong to pursue a young mother when all he wanted was a few laughs and some hot kisses. Nothing serious. And nothing permanent.

He'd learned his lesson about that back in college. Back then, he'd been deeply in love and engaged to be married. The relationship had blown up in his face and he wouldn't be going there again.

So when he learned that Evy was a mom, he'd decided to forget about her.

Too bad forgetting Evy Roberts was easier said than done.

He couldn't forget Evy.

Couldn't stay away, either. For the last few months, he'd been stopping by Doug's a couple of times a week just to see her, to hear her voice, to watch the warm, efficient way she dealt with her customers, the way she managed to be gracious and fun and no-nonsense all at the same time.

He liked everything about her. And he'd started thinking, well, so what if she had a little girl? He could work with that. Take it one day at a time. Just see how things went. Keep it fun and casual.

It didn't have to be a big deal. If nothing else, they might become friends.

Which was why tonight, he was through holding back. Tonight he would make a real move, at last.

Rising, he pushed in his chair and followed at a distance as she carried an empty serving tray to the end of the bar next to the famous haunted stool. She slid the tray onto the bar and signaled Doug that she had drink orders for him to fill.

But the bar owner was busy pouring beer for a couple of talkative cowhands. Evy should have time to exchange a few words.

If Wes could strike the right tone, he might convince her to meet up with him during Red, White and Bronco—they could get together at the rodeo tomorrow or at the barbecue on the Fourth. No pressure, just hanging out, getting to know each other.

Casual. Fun. No big deal.

He was directly behind her, about to step up beside her and turn on the charm. He knew this was it. He would make it happen at last. Before Doug turned to take Evy's order, he intended somehow to magically convince her that they needed to get to know each other better.

Hey, fortune favored the bold, right? And Wes was a pretty fast talker.

He'd just opened his mouth to say something charming when the window on the other side of the Death Seat shattered. A fist-sized object came hurtling through it.

Right at Evy.

Chapter Two

Wes lunged, grabbing for her.

A startled cry escaped her as he took her down, twisting his body so she wouldn't hit the edge of the bar as they fell. He felt a hard blow to the shoulder as they toppled to the floor—where he ended up on top of her.

"Oof!" She stared up at him, stunned.

He realized he was crushing her. "Sorry…" Bracing up on his hands, he blinked down at her. "Are you okay?"

"I, um…" They stared at each other. The bar had gone dead silent—someone must have unplugged the jukebox.

A rough voice barked, "My God, what was that?"

"A rock!" cried another voice.

"It came through the window!" shouted some-one else, a woman.

"Who in the ever-lovin' hell would do that?"

"Somebody could get hurt, for crying out loud!"

"Outside! Let's get'im, boys!"

Boots pounded the floor as several men ran for the door.

Wes and Evy, though? They were having a mo-ment. He gazed into her eyes, felt her softness be-neath him, and didn't care in the least that chaos had erupted all around them. He just wanted to lie here on the scuffed, grubby floor, staring into those wide green eyes.

A drop of blood fell onto her white shirt just above the soft swell of her breast. Another followed, deepest red against the white. Her glance shifted— from his eyes to her shirt and then up to him again. She gasped. "Your shoulder..."

He followed her gaze to where the rock had hit him. The blow had torn his shirt and broken the skin beneath it. "It's nothing. I'm okay." Lifting back and onto his knees, he held out a hand—and it happened again. She met his eyes and every-thing stopped.

Vaguely, he registered the continued commotion. Someone asked if they were all right as boots pounded back in from outside.

A man bellowed, "Whoever threw that rock is long gone!"

"Call the police!"

"Done." That was Doug's voice. "They're on the way."

"We should probably get up," Evy suggested, ending that second weirdly intimate moment where the two of them stared at each other in absolute silence as confusion reigned around them.

"Give me your hand."

Her soft palm met his. Their fingers meshed, hers cool and soft, his roughened by ranch work. A few bills slid from her apron as he pulled her to her feet.

He had to let go of her hand to bend, grab them up and return them to her.

"Thank you." She dropped them back into her apron pocket.

"Are you okay?" He wanted to touch her face, smooth her shining hair, run his palms down her body—reassure himself that she hadn't been hurt.

"I'm fine, Wes—thanks to you." She glanced at the shards of glass scattered under the window. "There's broken glass everywhere. Did you get any cuts?"

"Just where the rock got me."

"We need to patch that up. The first aid kit's in back." She turned toward the other end of the bar, pulling him along behind.

They got about two steps before Doug stopped them. "Everlee, you hurt?" His wiry gray eyebrows drew together in concern at the sight of the blood on her shirt.

"I'm fine. It's Wes's blood, not mine. He grabbed me just before that rock hit me."

Doug pulled her into a quick hug.

She insisted, "Really, I'm okay."

Taking her by the arms, Doug held her away. His dark gaze ran over her. "Just making sure." Finally, he nodded at Wes. "Sorry, son. That wound looks nasty."

Wes lifted his good shoulder in a half shrug. "It's not that bad," he said just as someone jostled him from behind.

"Hold on, everyone!" Doug shouted. "Stand back!" Several customers had moved in to get a closer look at the broken window, the scattered bits of glass and the rock that had caused all the commotion.

"What's that?" a customer demanded. "Looks like there's a note tied around that rock."

"Leave it," Doug commanded. "Don't anybody touch anything till the police get here." He nodded at Evy. "Go on. Patch him up."

"Will do. This way, Wes." She took his hand again and started walking.

Way too happy about how this was playing out, he followed her around to the pass-through at the other end of the bar, through the door to the kitchen to a storage area and, finally, into a cramped break-room with a small table and three chairs.

"Have a seat," she instructed.

He took a chair as she rummaged in the cabinet above the small steel sink until she found a white kit with a red cross on the top. She set the kit on the table and dragged the trash bin out from under the sink.

After washing her hands, she claimed the chair nearest him. "You're going to have to take off that shirt."

He popped the pearl snaps and eased it off his bad shoulder, holding it up to assess the damage. "Looks like some mean critter chewed on it." He hung it on the chair back.

"It's a nice one, though." She opened the kit and took out a handful of large disinfecting wipes. "Matches your eyes." She met his gaze for a half a second before she got busy tearing the wrapper off a wipe.

"You noticed my eyes, huh?" He sat back a little in the chair. A pretty blush had darkened her cheeks, but she didn't reply. He bit the inside of his lip to keep from grinning. She was all business, dabbing at the wound with the medicated wipe. He watched her slender fingers as she tended to him. "It's really not all that bad."

"Bad enough," she replied in a worried tone. "At least it's almost stopped bleeding—you're already bruising, though."

"I can see that."

"I hope it doesn't hurt too much." She freed another wipe and cleaned the area again.

"Evy…"

She glanced up sharply. "Ahem. Hmm?"

"I'm okay. It's not a big deal."

She looked at him again, her plush mouth twisted, her eyes enormous in her delicate face. "You got hurt instead of me…"

It was his moment and damned if he didn't seize it. "But look on the bright side…"

She glanced at him sideways. "There's a bright side?"

"Oh, yeah. Now you can make it up to me."

This close, he could hear her breath catch. "H-how?"

"Go out with me." His voice was a low growl. He wished she'd never stop dabbing at him with that wipe. And how did she manage to smell so good after racing around Doug's all evening serving beer, fries and nachos? He could sit here in this cramped space with her forever, just the two of them, nice and cozy.

"Wes, really, I—"

"Tomorrow night," he cut in before she could finish. "Let me buy you a big, juicy steak at DJ's Deluxe—and don't say you have to work. I know you get Sundays and Mondays off."

"Wes, I told you months ago that I don't date. I really don't have time for any of that."

"You should make time. You work too hard. Someone should spoil you a little."

"Spoiling is the last thing I need." She tried to look stern.

"Not true. You need more fun in your life."

She scoffed. "And you think you're going to help me with that?"

Damn. He wanted to kiss her. He couldn't wait to taste those soft lips for the first time. "Haven't you heard? I'm the master of fun."

She wore the cutest expression. Like an exasperated schoolmarm. "Did you not hear what I just said? I don't date."

"It's one night. Live a little. Evy Roberts, when are you going to let me show you a good time?"

Weston's question hung in the air between them as Evy got out the gauze, antibiotic ointment and adhesive tape. She felt confused—and excited, too.

He had her all turned around. She felt so powerfully drawn to him—and no way could she afford the distraction he represented.

She had so much she wanted to do in her life. She wanted more, for herself and her daughter. She longed to make her bighearted, generous dad proud of her. And despite her second discouraging sit-down with a loan officer last week, she still had her dreams. Someday she would live them.

And getting sidetracked by Wes Abernathy was not, nor could it ever be, on her to-do list.

She shook her head at him. "Please. The last thing I need in my life is a good time with the *master of fun*."

"Evy…"

"Stop." She held up the first aid kit scissors between them and snipped them open and shut, hard. "I'm a single mom with a four-year-old daughter. You and I have nothing in common." That ought to give the man pause.

But he only grinned that sexy grin of his. "You'd be surprised. Kids love me. My little niece, Maeve, is my biggest fan. And where is the rule that says a single mom shouldn't have a good time now and then?" He looked at her so intently now, as though it really mattered to him that she hear him out, give him a chance. "Just tell me, Evy. Is it Lola's father? Are you still in love with the guy?"

"So then." She gave him a wary look. "You know about my daughter?"

He only shrugged. "Yeah. I asked around about you. That was back last summer after the first time you brushed me off." As she tried to decide whether to be flattered or annoyed with him, he asked again, "So. Still in love with Lola's dad?"

Her breath had somehow gotten stuck in her chest again, the way it too often did around him. She drew herself up, stared him square in those sexy blue eyes and answered honestly. "That's long over—and the truth is, looking back now, sometimes I wonder if I was ever in love with him."

As soon as the words got out, she wished she could call them back. She had nothing to hide. However, what had gone on between her and Lola's dad was none of this rich cowboy's business.

She applied ointment to a thick pad of gauze, pressed it to his shoulder and began taping it in place. As she worked, she had to constantly remind herself that this…*thing* she had for this man just had to stop. She'd been fantasizing about him for months now. She was never going to do anything about it. Because she wasn't ready for love right now. She had way too much she needed to accomplish in life before she tried to make a relationship work again. She needed to put Weston Abernathy completely from her mind.

Too bad that each time she saw him, she only felt more drawn to him. Everything about him got to her—the ocean-blue eyes, the thick brown hair, the devilish grin. The way he looked at her, like she was so special, like he wanted to take her hand and twine his fingers with hers and stroll off into the sunset, just the two of them, side-by-side. He was pure temptation. The same as Lola's father, Chad, had been, a confident man with plenty of money, the guy that all the girls wished they could be with.

It was just a fantasy. Not real. She didn't need the fantasy. Someday, maybe, she would find a man of substance. Someone like her dad, who gave his all for the ones he loved.

But the "master of fun" as he called himself? The charmer all the girls were after? No, thank you. Not again.

She really shouldn't be alone with him. The attraction was just that powerful. It was downright unfair how amazing he looked without his shirt. She could stare forever at the way his hard, bare chest tapered so perfectly to his narrow waist.

And she had no excuse—none whatsoever—to be fascinated by the trail of silky-looking dark hair leading down between his pectoral muscles to disappear beneath the buckle of his belt.

Honestly, what was the matter with her? She felt almost dizzy just being so close to him.

"Have dinner with me," Wes commanded, his voice hushed, a little rough, thrilling.

"I told you—"

"We can go early. You can bring Lola, too."

She sucked in a slow breath. "Really, Wes. It's a bad idea. It can't go anywhere between us."

"Who said it has to go somewhere? I like you. I think you like me. We've got…a connection. Sparks. Don't even try to deny it. You feel this thing we've got going on between us."

"There is no 'thing.'"

"Liar." Now his voice was an intimate rumble. "Come on. Take a chance. Let's find out where all this chemistry leads us."

"It's a bad, bad idea."

"It's a great idea, Evy."

"No, Wes. I really can't."

He was silent after that. Apparently, he'd finally accepted that she would not be giving in to him.

Which was wonderful. Terrific. Exactly what she wanted—even though she felt glum suddenly, glum and thoroughly disappointed.

But then, as she closed the first aid kit, he said, "All right. I'll see you tomorrow at the rodeo."

She rose, the kit in her hands. "I doubt we'll be going."

Wes grinned up at her. "I'll be lookin' for you."

"Do you ever give up?"

He gave one slow shake of his head. "Uh-uh. Not when I really want something."

Evy said nothing.

What more was there to say?

He put on his shirt. She put the kit away and led him back out to the bar, where two Bronco PD officers had arrived and it was still much too quiet.

Wes went off to join his brothers.

"Is he all right?" Doug asked her as Wes walked away.

"He's going to be fine. What's happening?"

Doug flipped his bar towel onto his shoulder. "Turns out that *was* a note tied around the rock that almost hit you. The note says, *A Stone You Won't Forget.*"

"I don't get it. Should that mean something special to someone?"

"Not a clue. But the officers are very serious, They're taking nothing for granted. One of them announced that they have zero tolerance for this kind of violence. They're interviewing everyone, even Winona."

"Well, that's all good, right?"

"Sure. But personally? I don't think they're going to find any answers. I'm blaming the Death Seat."

She rolled her eyes. "Doug. Nobody was sitting on that stool."

"Exactly. Even with no one sitting on it, the Death Seat strikes again."

Evy shook her head. "You don't really believe that."

Before Doug could reply, one of the officers stepped up to the bar. "Everlee Roberts?"

"That's me."

"I'll need you to have a seat. I've got a few questions. This shouldn't take long."

Ten minutes later, Evy went back to work. The police left and the music started up again. People drank and danced and played pool.

And not once for the rest of the evening did she let her gaze stray in Weston's direction.

The next morning, when Evy entered the big kitchen in the ranch-style house on Union Street where she'd grown up, she found her dad, Owen, sitting at the breakfast table alone. His reading glasses had slipped down his nose and the Bronco Bulletin lay open on the table in front of him.

"Morning, Dad."

"Hey, sunshine…"

Evy went to the coffeepot and poured herself a cup. "Lola still in bed?" She turned and leaned back against the counter for that first perfect sip.

"Nope. She got up with me as usual." He folded his paper and set it aside as Evy took the chair next to him. He reported, "She ate a scrambled egg and a pancake, drank all her orange juice and now she's in her room trying to decide what to wear to the rodeo."

Yes, Evy had lied to Weston last night. She and Lola were going to the rodeo. Lola couldn't wait. "How long has she been getting dressed?"

Owen shrugged. "A while."

Lola loved to get dressed. She liked deciding which outfit to wear and then putting it on all by herself. Sometimes, though, she became frustrated with the complexities of clothing. She got stymied by buttons and snaps. Evy tried to be there to assist her as needed. "I'll just go check and see how she's doing."

Her dad shook his head. "She'll be fine for a few more minutes."

Something in his voice alerted her—excitement maybe? "Okay, Dad. What's going on?"

Owen clucked his tongue. "So suspicious." His cell phone sat beside him on the table. He poked at it and then slid it over so that she could see the screen, which was open to an entry in his bank account.

"Whoa." Stunned, she looked up to meet his gleaming hazel eyes. "A hundred and fifty thousand dollars? Did you rob a bank?"

He chuckled. "I sold my *Captain America*, number one."

Evy gasped. Her dad might be a semiretired plumber by trade, but his passion was collecting memorabilia—classic comic books and movie merch, mostly. "Oh, Dad. You didn't."

"Yes, I did."

She could not believe it. Released in 1941, the first-ever Captain America comic had Cap punching out Hitler on the cover. Her grandfather had bought it when it came out. Gramps had read it repeatedly. It wasn't in perfect condition. On the industry-standard 10-point grading scale for collectible comics, her dad's copy came in at 6.0, not high enough to sell for just under a million as a 9.4 once had, but worth a lot, nonetheless.

She could not believe he'd let it go. "That comic was your prized possession."

"And because of it, you're going to make your old dad proud. You're going to open Cimarron Rose."

The store she'd dreamed of creating since she was not much older than Lola would be a little bit boho and a whole lot cowgirl. And Evy was pretty much ready to go with it. She had a business plan. She knew which distributors and wholesalers she wanted to buy from. She understood her customer base, had a website design ready to launch and a marketing program all laid out. She just needed capital. So far, two local banks had turned her down.

As for the frustrating, wonderful man sitting next to her at the table, he'd offered to back her more than once in the past. She'd always refused to let him spend more money on her. "How many ways can I say it? You've already done so much. You're not using your hard-earned savings to make my career dreams come true."

"But, Everlee…" He tapped the screen of his phone with his index finger. "This money here, it's not savings. It's what you call a windfall. If it vanished tomorrow, I wouldn't even notice it was gone."

"Oh, yes, you would. And you already miss your *Captain America*, number one, now, don't you?"

"Not a bit."

She puffed out her cheeks with an exasperated breath. "You're lying. We both know it."

He shrugged his burly shoulders. "Well, it's gone now. I can't get it back. Good thing you can make me glad I sold it."

"No, Dad. I'm not—"

"Mommy!" Lola came bouncing in from the hallway that led back to the bedrooms. She wore a froth of red tulle for a skirt, a white, short-sleeved button-up shirt embroidered with sunflowers, a blue vest sprinkled with sewn-on stars and her favorite pink cowboy boots. The ensemble might not have much rhyme or reason, but Lola, with her big green eyes, long, wavy, almost black hair and excess of sass made it work in the most adorable way. She threw her arms wide. "Ta-da!"

Evy nodded in approval. "You look amazing!"

"Beautiful," Owen agreed.

Lola wrinkled her upturned nose. "There's just one thing…" She took the sides of her vest, pulled them wide and pouted. "The buttons got all wrong."

A closer look proved that Lola had managed to button only two buttons—neither of them in the corresponding buttonhole. "Would you like me to help you?"

Lola considered, frowning, sighing, tipping her head from side to side. "I really 'fer to do it myself." Lola loved words like *prefer*—words she considered grown-up words.

Evy took care to show no hint of a smile. This was serious business, after all. "Go for it, then."

"Well, I've been *trying* and *trying* and I think I tried enough. So yes, Mommy. Please button me up."

Evy dropped to a crouch and quickly corrected the problem. "There you go."

"Thank you. I can tuck it back in myself."

"Of course." Evy rose and grabbed her empty coffee mug.

Lola gazed up at her, a frown crinkling her forehead. "You better get dressed. We have to go very soon."

"We have time yet. The gates don't open till noon."

Lola widened her eyes and put on her most serious expression. "We need to go early before it gets crowded."

Evy dropped a kiss on her daughter's plump cheek. "Nice try." Mug in hand, she headed for the coffeepot.

Wes's almost-two-year-old niece, Maeve, bounced on his lap. "Horsie! Pwetty!" she cried and pointed a plump finger at the action below, where Charity John, in spangled red, white and blue, holding Old Glory high, rode a snow-white Arabian around the ring. Maeve giggled and clapped her hands in excited approval.

Next to Wes on the right, Callie Sheldrick, Maeve's soon-to-be stepmom, leaned close to Maeve's daddy, Tyler, who sat on Callie's other side. Tyler whispered something in Callie's ear. Callie laughed and kissed him. On Wes's other side, his brother Dean and his fiancée, Susanna Henry, appeared to be sharing secrets of their own.

Garrett, wearing his usual severe expression, sat on the far side of Dean. Crosby, down the row on the other side, stomped his feet and whistled as the new Miss Bronco finished circling the arena on her white horse.

All around Wes and his family, in the row behind and in front of them, sat the Hawkins women. They were nothing short of rodeo royalty. Outspoken seventysomething Hattie, the matriarch of the family, had been widowed young and worked the rodeo circuit much of her life. She had four daughters, all in their fifties now, all adopted—Josie and Hollie, who were Black; Suzie, who was white, and, Lisa, who was Latina. Hattie's four daughters had grown up working the rodeo with their mother. The Hawkins Sisters, as they billed themselves, became big stars. All four of the sisters had children of their own, some adopted, some born into the family.

Two of Hattie's granddaughters, Audrey and Brynn, were slated to compete in roping and barrel racing today.

"Oh, yes we are definitely thinking it over!" announced Hattie in response to something her daughter Hollie had said.

Weston had no idea what she meant. Neither did Crosby, who asked, "You're thinking *what* over?"

Hattie laughed, a bold, bigger-than-life sound. "We're considering making Bronco our home," she replied.

Josie, her eldest daughter, explained, "'We' means

the entire Hawkins family. It's not for sure yet, but we just might be settling in Bronco."

"We like it here," said Lisa. "And it's about time we found the right place to make a permanent home."

"Bronco has a lot going for it," declared Susie. "Geoff Burris loves it here and so do his brothers." Geoff was a rodeo legend now, the biggest star to hit the circuit in a generation. He was also a Bronco native, a hometown hero since he'd brought the Mistletoe Rodeo to town last year. As for Geoff's brothers, they were competing today, too.

About then, down below, an announcer brought on the mayor, who made a little speech reminding everyone not to forget the big barbecue tomorrow. After that, the show kicked into high gear with the first cowboy out of the chute riding bareback on a bucking bronc.

Weston enjoyed the spectacle, but kept one eye out for Everlee. Yeah, she'd as good as said she wouldn't be here today. So what? She might change her mind. Wes liked to think positive. The way he saw it, a negative attitude never helped a man get what he wanted.

An hour later, long after he'd handed Maeve back to Callie, he still hadn't spotted Evy. He was growing impatient. He wanted to make a blush bloom on her soft cheeks again. He wanted to hear her get all insistent that they couldn't. They shouldn't. Really, she simply *wouldn't*.

He didn't believe any of her excuses. She wanted him and he wanted her. This thing between them only kept getting stronger. In the end, they would both surrender to it.

And when it happened, it would be good between them. It would be great. He really liked Evy and wanted to be with her for as long as it lasted. The way he saw it, two people could have something special together even if it didn't last until the end of time.

As the announcer declared the winner in the saddle bronc riding event, Weston rose from his seat between his future sisters-in-law. He worked his way along the row to the nearest set of stairs.

From there, he climbed to the top and circled the arena by way of the aisle behind the last row of seats. As he walked, he scanned the closely packed stands anticipating his first sight of Evy in the crowd.

He spotted the little girl first—in the bench seats high up in the stands, directly across from where he stood. A miniature version of Evy, the child wore a red hat, a sequined vest and a red skirt of some puffy material, like a ballerina. Cutest thing he'd ever seen. He locked eyes on the child and there, right next to her, was the woman he couldn't stop thinking about.

The warm, sunny day suddenly seemed even brighter than before.

Chapter Three

Evy didn't see Weston until he started down the
row toward where she and Lola sat.

Before she could decide what to do next, he was
standing above her, looking much too lean and
manly for her peace of mind. How did he manage
to be so effortlessly hot? That smile of his could
coax a girl to suddenly decide that she needed to
make a few bad choices, develop some terrible habits, risk her poor heart again and probably lose it
for real this time.

Chapter Three

Evy didn't see Weston until he started down the
row toward where she and Lola sat.

Before she could decide what to do next, he was
standing above her, looking much too lean and
manly for her peace of mind. How did he manage
to be so effortlessly hot? That smile of his could
coax a girl to suddenly decide that she needed to
make a few bad choices, develop some terrible habits, risk her poor heart again and probably lose it
for real this time.

"What a surprise." He tipped his white Stetson.
"You decided to come to the rodeo, after all."

"Uh, yes, we did," she heard herself answer as

she desperately tried to think of a way to get rid of him—while at the same time secretly longing to elbow the stranger to her left until he slid over a little so that Wes could sit down.

Weston didn't wait for her to gather her scattered wits. He simply glanced at the man she'd almost poked with her elbow—and just like that, the stranger scooted sideways.

"Thanks." Wes took the empty space. The stranger grunted, knocked back a big sip from his giant red cup and refocused his attention on the action below. Wes said, "I'm here with my brothers so I can't stay long, but I did want to say hi."

Before Evy could reply, her daughter piped up with, "Hi, I'm Lola!" She offered her little hand and it disappeared in Wes's big one as they shook across Evy's lap.

"So good to meet you, Lola." Wes actually managed to sound like he meant that. "My name is Weston. You're looking very pretty today."

Lola loved a compliment. She beamed at Wes as she retrieved her hand and folded it with the other in her lap. "Thank you. I like blue and red and yellow. I like them a lot. I like *all* colors."

Wes gave a slow nod. "I do, too."

About then, Lola suddenly shifted her gaze to Evy. A tiny frown creased the space between her eyebrows. "Mommy?"

"Hmm?"

"Is it okay to talk to a stranger if you're here with me?"

Evy gave herself a mental shake and answered in an even tone. "Yes. As long as I'm with you, it's perfectly fine. Wes is a…friend of mine. I know him from Doug's."

"O-kay!" Lola straightened her frothy tulle skirt as everyone in the stands started clapping and stomping in reaction to the first calf roper's excellent time. Lola clapped and shouted, "Yay!" right along with the rest of them. Evy doubted her daughter had any idea what had just happened down in the dirt, but Lola always enjoyed making noise.

Wes leaned closer. "She's adorable."

"Thank you."

Lola shouted, "Yay!" again, followed by another burst of clapping. Then she leaned across Evy and asked Wes, "Are you from Bronco?"

"I am, yes. My family and I own a ranch."

"In Bronco Valley?"

"Bronco Heights."

"My mommy and me live in Bronco Valley with my pop-pop. Pop-Pop's a plumber. He fixes pipes. Do you have any broken pipes, Weston?"

"Not at the moment, no."

Evy leaned close to her daughter. "Don't monopolize the poor man, sweetheart."

"Monopo-huh?"

"I mean, why don't we let Weston watch the rodeo?"

Lola beamed her most angelic smile. "Okay, Mommy. Let's watch the rodeo."

Her silence lasted about a minute and a half. And then once again she was chattering nonstop, acting like she and Weston were long-lost best friends. Wes answered right back and didn't seem bothered that Lola wouldn't stop talking.

In fact, he seemed to be having a great time.

Lola shared way more than Wes ever needed to know. "My pop-pop has a girlfriend. Her name is Dotty Brock. She lives across the street from our house. Pop-Pop and Dotty have been friends for a long, long time. And now they are *more* than friends and sometimes they kiss each other."

"I know exactly what you mean, Lola."

Lola suddenly seemed unsure that *she* knew what she meant. "You do?"

"Yes. Sometimes a friend can become a girlfriend. My brother Dean was good friends with Susanna Henry for a long time. Now they are much more than friends. They're engaged to be married."

Lola stared, wide-eyed at that news. In a moment, she would come up with a fresh topic and be off and jabbering again.

Evy advised, "Wes, just tell her you want to watch the rodeo."

He only grinned. "Are you kidding? I need to know everything Lola wants to share with me."

And Lola had plenty to share. "Weston, I love to read. Mommy takes me to the *lie-berry* all the time to get more books from Miss Shari, who is the *lie-berrian* for children. And then I have daycare. It's fun. I go three times a week. Also, I want a puppy. I do. So much! Mommy and Pop-Pop say I'm not old enough yet, but I *am*…" Her voice trailed off as she frowned, deep in thought. Finally, she smiled. "But then sometimes I think what I *really* want is a kitten."

"It's a difficult choice," Wes agreed.

"Yes. Very *difficult*. And that's why I just can't decide."

"Lolly, honey, we need to let Weston get back to his brothers." In a firm voice, Evy interrupted the love-fest between the hot rancher she was *not* going out with and her little girl.

"Why?" Lola looked doubtful.

"Just take my word for it. We do." Evy aimed a determined smile at Wes. "How's your shoulder feeling?"

Oh, the way he looked at her, like he couldn't wait to spend more time with her. Private time. Intimate time… "My shoulder's fine. Until you mentioned it, I'd forgotten all about it."

"Well." She leaned closer and lowered her voice so that Lola wouldn't hear and start asking more questions. "Thank you again for getting between me and that rock."

"You're welcome—and you're right. I do need to get back. But before I go, let's talk about that dinner date you promised me." He said that loud and clear.

And Lola piped right up with, "Mommy, let's meet Weston at the barbecue tomorrow and then we can all stay to watch the fireworks together. Weston, the barbecue and fireworks are in Bronco Park, and I can't wait!"

"That's a terrific idea, Lola." His gaze stayed locked on Evy. "I'll be there and I'll come looking for you. Two or so? Save a seat for me?"

Evy knew she should say no—but she longed to say yes.

As she dithered over her reply, Lola spoke right up. "My pop-pop and Dotty will be there, too."

"Great." Wes grinned. "I'm looking forward to meeting them."

Evy felt herself weakening, what with both of them putting the pressure on her simultaneously. "See you at two, then."

He leaned close. She felt his warm breath on her cheek. "Did you just say yes to me?"

"It's only a picnic, Wes."

"But you did say yes."

She gave it up. "I did. But I can't say for certain where we'll be sitting. Sometimes it's hard to get a picnic table."

"One way or another, I will find you."

Why did she like the sound of that so much? "You are very determined."

"Bet on it." He rose. "See you tomorrow."

"Bye-bye, Weston!" Lola gave him a big wave. "See you at the barbecue!"

Evy watched him work his way along the row until he reached the next aisle. Then she made herself focus on the show down below. She kept thinking about him, though, second-guessing herself, feeling alternately eager to see him tomorrow and absolutely certain she was making a big mistake to encourage the guy in any way.

As they did every year, Weston, his brothers and his parents got to Bronco Park at midnight.

The family company, Abernathy Meats, had taken first place in the Fourth of July Barbecue contest last year. This year, they were all hyped up to do it again.

By the glow of tall LED lights spaced strategically around the area where the local ranchers set up their outdoor kitchens every year, the Abernathy family worked together like a well-oiled machine to set up prep and serving tables and get the smokers going. All around them, other Bronco families did the same. The specially seasoned beef would slow cook over hot, fragrant coals until four in the afternoon.

Once the meat was in the smokers, Wes and most of the family returned to the Flying A to get a few hours of sleep. This year, Crosby and Garrett had brought bedrolls. They would keep an eye on the smokers through the night.

Wes and the rest of them got back to the park at noon. Susanna and Callie came, too. They took turns looking after Maeve and pitched in wherever needed.

It was another fine day, sunny with a few cottony clouds floating around up there in the big blue bowl of the wide Montana sky. Wes wished he could make time speed up. Two o'clock couldn't come fast enough. He grinned every time he thought of Evy—and little Lola, too. That kid could talk a man's ear off.

By one, they pretty much had everything ready to go. Wes grabbed a cup of coffee from the thermal pitcher his mom always set up for barbecues, along with one of the muffins she'd brought to keep them going until the smokers finished working their magic. He found an empty camp chair and demolished his muffin. He was enjoying his coffee when Garrett took the chair next to him.

Divorced from his high school sweetheart for years now, Garrett wasn't what anyone would call a happy man. He worked hard and he took life seriously—too seriously, if you asked Weston or any one of their other three brothers. Garrett seemed most content when left alone.

Not today, though. He kept eyeing Wes as though he had something important to say.

Wes stuck his coffee in the holder on the arm of his chair. "What? Go ahead, put it on out there."

"Fine. I spotted you sitting with Evy Roberts and her daughter yesterday. Be straight with me. You got a thing going with Evy now?"

Not yet. But I'm working on it. "I like Evy. Is that a crime?"

"She's got a little girl, Weston. I think you should consider that before you go breaking her heart."

Sometimes his big brother just flat pissed him off. "Didn't you already make your point about this at Doug's Friday night?"

"I tried. It's pretty clear now that you didn't listen."

"Let it go, Garrett."

"I just want you to consider the consequences of your actions."

"You think you're Winona Cobbs all of a sudden, staring into your crystal ball, predicting the future? Well, you're not. And as for breaking Evy's heart, I've got no intention of doing any such thing."

"Of course you don't. You never do." Garrett spoke quietly, for Wes's ears alone. "But you're my brother. I know you. You play it like it's all a big party, a fine old time. From the outside looking in, you and I are nothing alike. But deep down, we've got a whole lot in common. After what happened with Belinda Fae, you're not letting any woman get too close, not ever again."

Wes did not want to talk about his ex-fiancée. The woman had broken him, pure and simple. And he'd chased after her anyway. He'd begged her to come back to him, to give him one more chance. He didn't even like thinking about what a damn fool he'd been back then.

The main point was, that would never happen to him again.

But that didn't mean he and Evy couldn't have something special for as long as they were together.

He faced Garrett squarely. "You're out of line here and you need to ease up."

"All I'm saying is, you're all for fun and good times—and that's it. That's as far as it goes. Getting serious with someone is not in your game plan. A young single mother, well, she doesn't need some good-time guy. Evy Roberts has a lot to deal with, working nights and raising a child. She could get hurt and that wouldn't be right."

"Look, I *like* Evy. I'm not going to hurt her. I just want to get to know her better, spend some time with her. As for her little girl, we hit it off, me and Lola. I like being around her, too. How is that wrong?"

Garrett sat forward in the chair—and then sagged back. "Okay. I give. It's not *wrong*, exactly. But it could *go* wrong, and you know it."

Wes just looked at his brother, straight-on and steady. The seconds ticked by.

Finally, Garrett gave in. "All right. It's none of my business, I get that. I just needed to have my say about it."

"And so you did."

"Damn right."

"Fair enough. So now you can leave it alone, right?"

"I think you're making a big mistake, and I might end up having to knock a little sense into you if you mess up too bad. But for right now, I've said what I needed to say." Garrett rose. "I think I could use a cold drink." He turned for the table with the coolers beneath it.

His brother's word echoing unpleasantly in his head, Weston finished his coffee. Garrett was right about a lot of things. But Garrett didn't really get the whole picture. Wes had tried for months to forget about Evy Roberts. Hadn't happened.

Sometimes a man just had to go after what he couldn't stop wanting.

"Will you look at this," said Dotty with a bright smile. "An empty table sitting right here, waiting for us."

"It's a great spot." Owen grabbed his girlfriend in a quick side hug, dropped a kiss on the crown of her blond head and then glanced up at the thick canopy of leaves overhead. "Off by itself a little, shaded by a nice big oak."

Dotty, who had always reminded Evy of the mother in that old sitcom, *That '70s Show*, set her cute Amish-style picnic basket on one of the benches. "Let's get to work," she said briskly.

"I'll help!" chirped Lola.

Dotty gave a crisp nod. "I'm counting on it."

There wasn't all that much to do. Dotty had brought paper plates and plastic utensils, along with some snacks, her special-recipe baked beans and a big tub of coleslaw. They would buy drinks and dessert from the booths at the Red, White and Bronco Carnival Marketplace set up not far away. Barbecue and corn on the cob would be available from the ranchers who manned the smokers and grills across the picnic area from this perfect, shady spot.

They'd barely finished spreading the red-and-white-checked tablecloth and setting out the plates and plasticware when Lola started waving.

"Weston! Come see me!"

Evy's silly heart actually skipped a beat. She glanced over her shoulder and spotted the handsome cowboy she couldn't stop thinking about. He was headed straight for them.

"Afternoon, Lola." He tipped his hat.

"Weston! Hi!" Lola grinned so wide, Evy could almost see her tonsils.

Wes gave a nod to Owen and Dotty. "Folks." And then he turned to Evy. "You found a great table, I see."

"And you found *us*. Fast."

He smirked at her. "Told you I would."

Evy's dad came around the table, arm outstretched. She introduced them. The two men shook hands.

Owen said, "You're one of Hutch and Hannah's boys."

"Yes, sir. I am."

"Well, pleased to meet you, Weston. Call me Owen." Dotty moved in close and Owen wrapped his arm around her. "This is my girl, Dotty." He said it with pride and Evy felt a tug of equal parts joy and sadness.

Evy was twelve when Lola Vicario Roberts died

crossing the street, the victim of a distracted driver who'd blasted right through a red light. Sometimes, like now, the loss felt fresh, painfully new. Still, Evy had always liked Dotty, whose husband, Ned, had passed away three years after Evy's mom.

"Mommy." Her mother's namesake gazed up at her, anticipation in her eyes. "Can we go to the carnival now?"

"You young folks go on," Owen suggested.

Evy glanced up at Wes. He readily agreed. "The carnival it is."

An hour later, they returned to the table. Lola was triumphant, carrying a big stuffed sloth she'd named Fiona after the princess in her favorite movie, *Shrek*.

"Weston won it for me playing the water gun game," she explained proudly to her pop-pop and Dotty. Both Owen and Dotty agreed that Fiona was the finest-looking sloth they'd ever seen.

"Maeve!" Lola called out, waving. Tyler Abernathy and Callie Sheldrick were coming their way. Tyler had little Maeve in his arms.

Maeve waved a plump hand and shouted, "Woe-wa!"

Wes asked, "You know my niece, Maeve?"

"'Course, I do," said Lola. "Maeve comes to the *lie-berry*, too!"

Callie had a blanket. She spread it out on the

grass for Maeve and Lola. The little girls played together as the adults enjoyed the chips and salsa Dotty had brought and made small talk for a while.

At four, Weston, Tyler and Callie had to go help at the cookers, where the meat was ready at last. Wes returned alone at a little after five and sat with them as they ate. When the mayor announced the winners in this year's barbecue contest, Abernathy Meats took second place.

Wes didn't seem all that broken up. "There's always next year," he said with an easy shrug.

A little later, he went off to help load up the barbecue equipment so it would be ready to go at the end of the night. When he came back, he brought a cherry pie to share.

A five-piece band started playing over by the portable dance floor. Owen and Dotty danced. Wes alternated dancing with Lola and with Evy.

When he danced with Evy, he pulled her close. She breathed in his woodsy scent and tried not to think about how wonderful his lean arms felt wrapped around her.

He saved the fast ones for Lola, leading her in a sort of modified two-step, holding both her hands, keeping her close so she didn't get stepped on. Lola loved every minute of it. She giggled when he twirled her and talked his ear off the rest of the time, raising her voice to compete with the band.

It didn't seem at all fair that the man was so good with Lola. If Evy didn't watch herself, she could easily begin imagining a future with him. How that had happened so fast, she had no idea. After the enormous disappointment of her relationship with Lola's father, well, she really had planned to avoid getting close to a man until Lola was older and Evy had fulfilled her career dreams.

At first, with Lola's dad, Evy really had thought it was love. But looking back, she saw the sad truth. She'd been impressed by Chad Ames, swept off her feet by his sophistication and popularity. She was a small-town girl and he was a big man at the University of North Carolina, a Chapel Hill native from a wealthy family. He'd pursued her and won her.

Chad was her first, the only man she'd ever slept with. They'd dated exclusively. And then she'd missed her period.

She'd always been regular as clockwork, so she'd gone and bought herself a test. Chad took her to a doctor to confirm what the test had already proved—and then he sat her down and explained that being a father just wasn't part of his life plan right now. Evy had replied that the baby was coming whether it was in his life plan or not.

He hadn't argued with her. He'd just started pulling away. By the end of the semester, she rarely saw him. She'd had to accept that the two of them were through.

Eight months pregnant, she'd gone home for the summer after her junior year. Her doctor in North Carolina had ordered her not to travel alone, so her dad had come to drive her back. Chad had not objected to her leaving. In fact, when she'd called him to tell him she was going home, he'd seemed relieved. She'd never returned to Chapel Hill. Chad had missed his daughter's birth and never come to Bronco.

He'd set up a trust fund for Lola, but never once asked to see his child. Evy had gone to a lawyer and claimed full custody. No pushback from Chad. He signed the papers and sent them back. As a result of his disinterest, Lola had never met her dad or her grandparents on her father's side.

Evy found his behavior infuriating. And sad. And so disappointing.

And Evy simply didn't need any more disappointment in her life. She had her daughter and her dad and a good life in her hometown. Eventually, she would have the shop she'd always dreamed of.

It was enough for now.

She really didn't want to get all tangled up with a guy. Men were a distraction. Steering clear of them hadn't been difficult for her at all the past four years.

But then along came Wes.

He really did tempt her.

So what? She wasn't going to give in to that temptation. She wasn't going to date Wes—and she would never start having fantasies of forever with him.

And yet…

How could she keep her poor heart from yearning when he wrapped her close in his arms and they swayed to a cover of Rascal Flatts's "Bless the Broken Road"?

Overhead, the twilight sky glowed in layers of orange and purple. She felt his hand on her back, gentle but firm, and she longed for the very thing she kept promising herself she didn't need. She wanted just what he'd offered her on Saturday night—the chance to find out where this chemistry might take them.

Not much later, at full dark, the fireworks started.

Dotty, who always came prepared, spread a faded quilt on the grass and they all five sat together to watch the bottle rockets, fountains and Roman candles light up the night sky. Wes sat cross-legged—and Lola, clutching her stuffed sloth, climbed right into his lap. She kept almost dropping off to sleep, her dark head drooping like a flower on a slender stalk. And then another rocket would go screaming skyward and she would jerk awake and cry out, "Wow! Weston, look at that one!"

And he would agree that it was the best one yet.

Evy sat with them, behind her dad and Dotty.

After a while, she couldn't help thinking that surely Weston needed a break from her four-year-old by now. "Just pass her over here if your legs are going to sleep," she suggested.

He shook his head. "She's fine."

"But can you still feel your feet?"

He leaned a little closer. His mouth was right there, a few inches from hers. "So far, so good." She knew that he would kiss her.

She *wanted* him to kiss her.

But then a comet screamed skyward, exploding outward into a flower of blinding light. They both turned toward the brightness.

And the dangerous moment passed.

Lola slept on. The big day had finally worn her out. For the rest of the show, she didn't stir.

After the last flare of light died to darkness once more, Dotty turned around and whispered, "Aw. Lolly's conked out." She patted Evy's knee. "You sit tight for a bit. Let her sleep. Your dad and I will load up the car."

"Thanks," Evy whispered back.

A hush had seemed to fall over Bronco Park.

Everyone quietly went about gathering their things and loading up their vehicles.

Evy turned to Wes. "I'll take her now."

He just looked at her for several dreamy seconds, a soft look that sent a warm shiver dancing over her skin. Finally, he replied, "In a minute."

Again, she just knew that he would kiss her.

But he didn't lean closer. "The pet adoption at Happy Hearts Animal Sanctuary is tomorrow," he said.

Happy Hearts, a working farm, was owned and run by Daphne Taylor Cruise. The sanctuary offered pets for adoption every day of the year. But on July 5, Daphne put on an adoption party combined with the Favorite Pet Contest. Every animal—whether staying at the shelter or brought from home—was eligible to win a trophy. The point of the event was to find owners for as many of the rescued animals as possible, making room at Happy Hearts for more.

"I've been thinking about tomorrow night," Wes added with a determined gleam in his eyes.

She knew where this was going. "What about it?"

"I have it on good authority that Doug gave you tomorrow night off."

"I worked six days last week, so yeah. I have Tuesday off. How did you know that?"

"There was a schedule on the breakroom wall."

This man. Not only smoking hot and charming, but also far too observant. "Clever."

"I try to pay attention, to pick up all the clues, especially where you're concerned." He looked down at her sleeping daughter and then back up at Evy. "So here's my plan. At noon, I'll pick you and Lola up for the pet contest. We'll have a great time at Happy Hearts, the three of us. And then tomorrow night, you and I are going out for dinner at DJ's Deluxe."

"Just like that, huh?"

"Say yes."

"I don't know. It could be dangerous."

"How?"

"I have to consider Lola. She'll get ideas."

"About us?"

"Well, that, too. But I was thinking about Happy Hearts. Animals everywhere—and Lola wants a dog."

"*And* a cat."

"You do know you're making my argument for me, right?"

"Say yes, anyway."

"I don't know if I'm ready for a pet, which is why taking Lola to a pet adoption can't be wise."

"Evy." His voice was wonderfully rough, yet sweet and slow as honey. "Say yes."

She shouldn't. She knew it. And yet she was smiling. "Yes."

He didn't stop there. "Dinner, too."

It was only one date, she reasoned. One date didn't make them a couple. "I don't think—"

"*Yes*. Come on. Say it."

"I can't believe I'm doing this."

"Evy. Is that a yes?"

She gulped. And then, slowly, she nodded.

"I want to hear you say it."

"Yes."

His anticipation rising at just the thought of the day and evening ahead, Wes got to the Roberts house the next day at noon on the nose.

Owen, in workpants and a blue T-shirt with the name of his company, The Plumbing Professionals, stamped on the pocket, answered the door and invited him in. "Hope you're not in a hurry. Lola's still getting dressed."

"Pop-Pop, who's there?" the little girl shouted from somewhere down the hallway that branched off the one that led to the front door. "Weston, is that you?" Before he could answer, he heard Evy's voice, too, though she spoke more quietly and he couldn't make out the words. "Never mind!" Lola chirped. "We will be right out!"

"Let's hope she means that," said Owen wryly.

"This way…" He led Wes to a homey combination family room and kitchen. "Have a seat. Coffee?"

"No, thanks. I'm all set."

"Weston!" Lola appeared before he even had a chance to sit down. "All ready to go." Today, she wore blue jeans and a purple shirt with purple boots to match.

"Love your boots."

"Thank you." She gave him a coy smile.

And then Everlee appeared from the hallway. Her silky jewel-green shirt matched her eyes and she'd let her hair down. The dark waves tumbled past her shoulders. "Hi," she said.

He felt like the luckiest man on the planet. Finally, after months of dreaming about her, they were actually spending time together. Yesterday had been perfect.

And today would be even better.

At Happy Hearts, Daphne Cruise's squad of young helpers had set up rows of folding chairs in a big pasture between the barns and the house. Every chair had an occupant.

Daphne played master of ceremonies. Her helpers brought out the animals for the prospective pet owners to admire and Daphne said lovely things about each of them. She seemed to know every dog, goat, pig and cat personally.

Lola, sitting up straight in the chair between him and Everlee, kicked her purple boots, clapped her hands and fell in love with all of them. She would have adopted every critter at Happy Hearts if Evy had only said yes. Lola chattered away, sighing in delight and longing, clapping her hands all the louder when someone stepped up to take an animal home.

"And we have a special treat for all of you today," announced Daphne about an hour and a half into the show. One of the kids led a big puppy to the podium—a cute one with floppy ears and a brown spot over one eye. "Meet Archie. He's six months old and his mama is someone we all know and love."

Daphne launched into the story of Maggie, the border collie/Australian shepherd mix who had vanished last summer after winning the Favorite Pet Contest. Eventually, after stopping in with more than one resident of Bronco, Maggie had finally been brought back to Happy Hearts and reunited with her adoptive family—but not before delivering a litter of eight pups. All eight had quickly found homes.

"But things didn't quite work out for Archie," Daphne said. As if on cue, Archie looked up at her and let out a plaintive whine. She bent to give him a pat on the head before going on. "His adoptive family had to move to Chicago suddenly and they couldn't take Archie with them."

Lola couldn't bear it. "Mommy!" she stage-whispered. "We have to take him. He needs us so much!"

Wes glanced at Evy. He could see it all on her beautiful face. She wasn't ready to take on a puppy, but she was having trouble resisting the look of longing in her little girl's eyes.

Finally, Evy said quietly, "Let it go for now, Lolly."

Solemnly, Lola nodded. "But we can talk about it later, 'kay?"

Evy said nothing. Lola seemed to get the message, though. At least she let it go.

Daphne was still speaking. She talked of how traumatic it was for a pup to be brought back. "The good news is he's leash-trained *and* house-trained already. So please, think about giving Archie a home. But also be certain that you're ready to raise him and love him for all of his days."

No one jumped up to claim him. Wes didn't know what to think. Would the puppy be left behind again?

On a happier note, when the votes were tallied for the favorite pet, Archie won the prize. Everyone whistled and applauded at that news.

So why had no one claimed him?

As people got in line at the adoption tables and wandered off to tour the farm or enjoy a cold drink, Lola grabbed Evy's hand. "Mommy, Archie didn't get a home yet. I think he really does need us."

Evy slowly shook her head. "He'll find a home eventually. Until then, Daphne and her helpers will take excellent care of him. I'm sorry, Lolly. But we're just not ready for a puppy right now."

Lola looked about to cry. "Please, Mommy…"

Wes knew he should probably stay out of it. Evy was the parent here, after all. But he leaned close to her anyway and whispered in her ear. "Let me try talking to her?"

Evy sighed. "Sure. But gently, please."

"Absolutely." He crouched to get eye-to-eye with the little girl. "Lola, taking on a dog is a big step and you and your mom are very busy. You might not have time to give Archie the attention he needs. Plus, a dog like Archie comes from working stock. He's happiest when he has a job to do and room to roam."

Lola wrinkled her nose. "What's working stock?"

"It means Archie is the kind of dog that ranchers and farmers often raise to help take care of sheep or to herd cattle."

"So you mean Archie needs to live on a ranch?"

"Not necessarily, but a ranch or a farm is ideal for a dog like Archie. He needs to keep busy."

Lola blinked. "Weston. *You* have a ranch."

"Well, yes, but…"

Lola's eyes were big as Moon Pies now, shiny with tears of sympathy for the cute mutt who needed a forever home. "Weston, please. If I can't have him, will you *please* take him home? He needs you. He needs you so much. Just look at him." She threw out a hand in Archie's direction.

Wes knew he shouldn't look. But his head kind of swiveled around of its own accord. And there was that floppy-eared dog, staring right at him with those sweet, soulful eyes.

"Lola, I…" He faced the little girl again.

She said nothing. She didn't need to. Her hopeful, pleading expression said it all.

He glanced back at the dog. Archie whined and perked an ear.

Wes couldn't do it. He could not hold out against both the child *and* the dog. "All right. If Archie hasn't been adopted already, he's got a home with me at the Flying A."

Chapter Four

"Yes!" Lola reached for a hug. He was still crouched in front of her, so she had no trouble wrapping her little arms around his neck. "Thank you," she whispered fervently in his ear.

Evy looked a little misty-eyed when he rose and faced her. "You sure about this?"

"Hey. A cowboy can always use a good dog."

"Then I guess you need to head for the adoption table, huh?"

"Looks that way."

Lola was already moving on to her next request. "Is it okay if I pet Archie and then, Mommy, could we please go visit the barn where the kittens are?"

Earlier, Daphne had explained that at Happy Hearts mama cats and their kittens lived in a special area in one of the barns.

"Sure." Evy took her daughter's hand.

Wes lined up at the adoption table. Twenty minutes later, he had himself a sweet-faced, floppy-eared, half-grown puppy. He took Archie back to the rows of folding chairs and sat down. The pup dropped to his haunches beside him. Wes scratched him under the collar and wondered why anybody would return a sweet dog like this one, a pup that wanted to please and looked up at a man through big, soft, hopeful eyes.

"Don't you worry, boy," he said, bending close to the dog so his words wouldn't be heard by anybody else. "It's you and me now and I give you my solemn word that won't change. I was returned myself, you might say. By someone I loved very much. Someone I trusted completely. Didn't like it one bit. And I would never do a thing like that to you."

Archie made a low, sympathetic sound, like he understood, like he knew that he and Wes were now a team.

A moment later, Evy and Lola came out of the kitten barn. Evy had one of those cardboard cat carriers clutched in her hand.

"Weston!" Lola cried. "Come see, come see!"

"Let's go, boy." He clicked his tongue and Archie followed right along without a single tug on the leash.

"What's going on?" he asked when they met midway between the kitten barn and the adoption table.

"Mommy let us get a kitten!" Lola was over the moon.

Evy met Wes's eyes and gave him a sheepish smile. "What can I tell you? You took Archie and that got me thinking about all the pets that really do need homes. Then, in the barn, there were all these cute kittens, including this one little white one with a black tail and ears and a perfect heart-shaped black marking at the base of her spine. Wait till you see her. She's a complete sweetheart. I started thinking how a kitten isn't *that* much of a challenge. So I called my dad and he said why not and…" She dipped her head toward the cat carrier. "Here we are."

Lola demanded, "Mommy, you have to let Weston see her! She is so beautiful. The most beautiful kitten in the whole world ever!"

Evy turned to her daughter. "Lolly, remember how we talked about that, about how she's cozy in there now and opening and closing the cat carrier might frighten her?"

"But I want Weston to see her! He has to see her!"

Evy held firm. "And once we get home, he will."

"No, Mommy! I want to show Weston *now*." Lola had that same look Wes's niece, Maeve, got now and then when a tantrum was brewing.

Evy instructed quietly, "Lolly, you need to calm down."

Lola pleaded, "But, Mommy, I need to show Weston! I do, I really, really do!" Now she was crying. She stomped her booted feet, fisted her hands, threw back her wavy hair and let out a wail.

Somehow, Evy remained calm. "Stop, please." She kept her voice gentle but unwavering. "Take a big breath. Listen."

It surprised the hell out of Wes when Lola sniffled loudly, sucked in a big breath and pressed her lips together. Shutting her eyes tight, she nodded. "What?"

"Stop now. Think now. And then tell me that you are okay."

Lola sniffled some more. She dashed at her eyes with the back of her hand. Finally, she opened her eyes. "I am o-*kay*."

Evy gave her a slow, tender smile. "Very good." Kneeling, she set the cardboard carrier on the grass and held out her arms. "I would really like a hug."

Lola threw herself at Evy. They hugged it out. Finally, Evy tipped the little girl's chin up and said in a quiet voice, "This is the thing, Lolly. We don't want to scare the kitten. If I open this carrier and you are shouting and jumping up and down, that wouldn't be good for her. She's little and we're big and she doesn't know us yet. We're strangers to her and a little kitten can be afraid of strangers sometimes."

Lola nodded again. "Okay, Mommy. I won't show Weston until we get home."

"That's great. Thank you for being so understanding."

"It's okay," Lola replied, looking solemn. "But can I please pet Archie?"

Evy slanted Wes a questioning glance and he nodded at Lola. "Go for it."

Archie wagged his tail and panted with contentment as Lola stroked a hand down his back and scratched him behind the ears.

"Let's stop at a pet store. What do you say?" Wes asked as they turned onto Commercial Street. "I need a few things for Archie and I'm guessing you'll want to stock up on cat food and buy a litter box."

"Can we, Mommy?" Lola asked from her car seat in back.

After the near-meltdown at Happy Hearts, Evy had half expected Weston to suddenly decide he needed to get home to the ranch ASAP. But instead, he was offering to stop for pet supplies. Evy couldn't help thinking she could get used to having him around.

With a grateful smile, she answered, "Yes, please."

His grin lit her up inside. "Done."

"Yay!" shouted Lola. Archie made an anxious sound. The kitten stayed quiet. She'd cried for a minute or two when Wes started up his truck but had remained mostly silent during the drive.

At the pet store, they all went in together—including Archie and the kitten in her carrier. By the time they piled back into Wes's pickup, he'd stocked up on essentials for Archie and Evy had all the necessary kitten supplies.

A few minutes later, they arrived at the Bronco Valley house, where they brought in the dog, the cat and the cat supplies. Evy's dad had left a note on the kitchen counter to let her know he'd gone out on a call.

Together, Evy, Lola and Wes set up a kitty area in the big laundry room off the kitchen.

The kitten seemed surprisingly unfazed when they let her out of the carrier. She hissed at Archie once, but Wes told the puppy to sit and the dog obeyed.

"Good dog!" exclaimed Lola. She plunked down cross-legged on the laundry room floor, scooped up her kitten and cuddled her close.

Wes, on one knee a few feet away, petted the puppy and praised him some more.

"He really does seem well trained," said Evy, who leaned back against the washer. "A great dog."

"I know, right?" Wes gave the pup one of the treats he'd stuck in his pocket before they pulled out of the pet store parking lot. Archie sat up straight and proud, as though he understood that his new human thoroughly approved of him.

Lola demanded, "What should we name my kitten?" She set the little fur ball on the floor beneath the table Evy used to fold clothes. The cat sniffed at the litter box and then lapped from her water bowl.

Wes said, "That heart on her butt is really cute."

"Mommy said that's her *lower back*, Weston," Lola corrected.

"All right then, on her *lower back*. I have an idea. What about *Valentine* for a name, because of that heart?"

Lola wasn't sure. "Like Valentine's Day?" She'd traded valentines last February in daycare for the first time.

Evy asked, "Isn't Valentine a boy's name?"

Lola scooped her kitten close again and nuzzled her fur. "A boy's name won't work. My kitten is a *girl*."

Wes suggested, "Valentina, then?"

Lola tried it out. "Valentina…"

Evy offered, "Maybe Tina, for short?"

The kitten came strolling back to Lola. Purring, she rubbed herself against Lola's knee.

"Valentina. Tina, for short." Lola sat up straighter. "I *like* it." She gave the kitten one long, slow stroke from the top of her head to the end of her black tail. "Hey, Tina." The kitten purred louder. "Welcome home."

"Wow," Evy said as the host who had greeted them at the front podium led them to their table.

"You like it?" Wes asked, though he could see the answer in her smile.

"I do."

The host pulled back Evy's chair for her and handed them each a menu. "Your server will be right with you."

Wes thanked him and off he went.

Evy glanced up at the copper light fixture overhead. "Nice. This is DJ's Rib Shack kicked up about a dozen notches."

"It is. And the food is great, too." DJ's Deluxe was a big step up from the down-home DJ's Rib Shacks that had made the chain's owner, DJ Traub, famous. At the original Rib Shacks, they served the food on paper plates and customers sat at picnic tables. Rib Shack ribs were the best around, but the atmosphere was strictly casual.

DJ's Deluxe was another experience entirely.

The restaurant had an industrial vibe, with accents of brushed nickel, lots of hammered copper and a long teak bar polished to a high shine. Only the best-quality liquor and expensive wines lined the shelves behind it. Somehow, the restaurant managed to be warm yet upscale.

When their server came, Wes ordered a good sipping whiskey and he and Evy decided to split a nice bottle of wine. They ordered appetizers to share and steaks.

When the server went off to get their drinks, Evy said, "This is such a treat. Thank you, Wes."

"My pleasure." He felt like a couple million bucks right now, to be out with her at last after months and months of wanting her, telling himself that it wouldn't be a good idea, really—and then realizing he would never be satisfied if he didn't at least ask her out.

She laughed, a soft, thoughtful sound. "And you were so great today with Lola. She's always felt everything so deeply. She's got so much joy in her, but all that enthusiasm can lead to acting out now and then. We've been working on ways she can calm herself down when she gets overexcited."

"You're an amazing mom," he said, and meant it.

Her smile was so beautiful, glowing. And kind of shy, too. "Thank you. I don't always get it right with her. But I try."

The server came, presented Wes with his drink and uncorked the wine.

As soon as the woman left, Wes said, "Kids do get keyed up, especially when puppies and kittens are involved."

She shut her eyes and sighed. "I can't believe we now have a kitten to raise. What was I thinking?"

"That Valentina is too cute for words and you couldn't resist?"

She let out low laugh. "How'd you guess?"

"I've seen the kitten."

Evy sipped from her wineglass. She asked how Archie was settling in at the ranch.

"He's staying with Tyler and Callie right now, so he won't have to be all alone on his first night in a new place. Maeve's already in love with him."

"I have no doubt about that."

He watched her soft, full lips move and thought about kissing her. Really, that should be a priority—their first kiss. It needed to happen tonight.

The server came with the appetizers. They dove into the food, the conversation flowing as easily as the wine.

She talked about how her dad had started going to Doug's a lot when she was twelve, after her mom died suddenly. "My dad was so sad and lonely back then."

"I'm guessing you were, too."

"Yes. I was. But I slowly adjusted to losing her.

I wouldn't say I'll ever stop missing her, but the pain gets more bearable as the years go by. It was the same for my dad. Doug Moore helped my dad through the hardest time. Doug's a gentle, smart man with a wicked sense of humor and a big heart. He and my dad became friends and then, over time, I got to know Doug, too. Eventually, he hired me to wait tables at the bar. It's working out well for right now."

"And in the future?"

Before she gave him an answer, the server appeared, whisked away their empty appetizer plates and presented them with thick, juicy tenderloins and spicy steak fries.

Once they were alone again, Wes said, "I think I heard somewhere that you went to University of North Carolina."

She actually snickered. "You *heard somewhere*, huh?"

He confessed, "Well, I *might* have asked around about you. A little."

"Right."

"Or maybe a lot."

They shared one of those moments, full of anticipation and excitement. The air seemed to shimmer in the space between them. He looked in those eyes of hers and never wanted to look away.

Finally, she said, "I did go to UNC, made it

through my junior year on the Dean's List every semester. Then I came home and had Lola. I never went back." She peered at him more closely. "You have a thousand questions about Lola's dad, right?"

"Well, maybe not a full thousand. But I do kind of wonder what happened with him."

She ate a bite of her steak. "Okay, it's like this. Lola's dad really isn't in the picture. I have full custody. He's set it up so Lola will be taken care of financially, but he never comes to Bronco to see her and he never asks for her to go there."

"What a bastard."

She shrugged. "I find the whole situation disappointing more than anything. But Lola's what matters. She's everything to me and I wouldn't have her if I hadn't been with him. He gave me Lola, and I'm so grateful he did. I do worry about later, about how bad it will hurt her if her dad never wakes up and reaches out."

Wes didn't know what to say to that except, "Lola is something special. And she's got you. And your dad."

A soft smile curved her lips. "My dad is the best, I have to agree."

"I think you might be surprised how strong Lola is."

"I hope you're right."

They ate in silence for a few minutes and he

found himself wondering if they were getting in too deep. It was only a first date. Shouldn't they be talking about all the safe, surface things—favorite country bands and the Grizzlies versus the Bobcats?

No, he decided. He wanted to know everything about her. Not just the surface stuff. "You mentioned that your job at Doug's is great for now, but you didn't answer my question. What about your future?"

She sipped her wine. "You really want to hear my life story, huh?"

Yes, he did. "Something wrong with that?"

"I guess it depends."

"On?"

"Wes, I'm not ready for love and commitment, you know? I don't want to get too deeply involved with a guy."

He leaned in again and lowered his voice for her ears alone. "I don't want any of that, either. I'm all about right here and right now. And right now, every time I say goodbye to you, I'm already planning how I'll see you again. When I'm with you, I want to know all your secrets—or at least, all the ones you're willing to share with me."

"But you're not looking to get serious?"

"Nope."

"Why not?"

He hesitated over that one.

She asked, more softly, "Did someone...hurt you?"

Something about that question made him feel nothing short of pitiful—and yet, he saw sincere interest and honest curiosity in her eyes. What could he do but man up and give it to her straight? "Yeah. We were engaged. Her name was Belinda Fae Whitlock. I met her in college, Texas A&M."

"You and Belinda met in college—like me and Chad."

"Yes, we did." He had no desire to talk about Belinda right now—or ever, for that matter. But Evy had laid it right out there about Lola's father. He felt he owed her a little truth in return. "It's been more than a decade since it all blew up with Belinda. I can honestly say I am completely over her."

Evy set down her fork and eased her long, slim hand across the table. He put his on top of it, engulfing it. Her hand felt so soft and delicate in his, her skin like velvet, cool and pleasurable to the touch.

"You really don't like taking about her." It wasn't a question.

He gave a humorless chuckle. "Let me put it this way. Talking about Belinda beats tangling with a polecat, but not by much."

She laughed and tossed her head. Her long black hair shimmered with glints of deep red in the light from the copper fixture above their table. He stared at the silky column of her neck and thought about putting his lips there, flicking out his tongue, tasting her...

"Your steak will get cold," she whispered, and eased her hand from his grip. He kind of hated to let it go.

They picked up their forks and focused on dinner, eating in mutual silence for a minute or two. Oddly, it wasn't uncomfortable, that silence. Far from it. He felt...stimulated. All his senses attuned.

She said, "As for my future, yes, I've got plans. I want to open a store in Valley Center."

Valley Center was the Bronco Valley shopping area. It included several streets south of Center Street, near Bronco Park. He listened, impressed, as Evy lovingly described her business plan and the shop she envisioned. "I even have a name for my store. Cimarron Rose."

"I like it—but Bronco Heights is a little more exclusive, more upscale. I'm surprised you don't want to open your store there."

"Bronco Heights is great," she agreed. "But I *love* Bronco Valley. It's my neighborhood. It's where I grew up. I want to build something of my own in my hometown. I want to support and contribute to the Valley Center business community. I just need the money to get things going. So far, the banks in town aren't interested. My dad is ready to back me, but of course I turned him down."

"Why *of course*?"

She set down her fork and picked up her wine. "Have you noticed we *live* with him? My dad's a rock. The best of the best. I just can't take any more from him. And now he's gone and sold his *Captain America*, number one, for me?" Her lower lip quivered and her eyes glittered with moisture. "Uh-uh. I just can't, I really can't. I—"

"Whoa." He reached across the table and captured her hand again. "Evy, what's wrong? What happened just now? Talk to me."

"Nothing." She was lying and he knew it. She looked away. "Everything's perfect. It's fine."

"Hey, now. Hey…" He kept hold of her hand—and she let him.

With a tiny sniffle, her head still turned away from him, she said softly, "Sorry. Really. I *am* okay."

"You're sure?"

"Mmm-hmm." She gave a tug on her hand.

He let it go then, and asked, "So, what was that about *Captain America*, number one?"

She launched into an explanation of her dad's love of old comic books, movie posters and action figures. "My dad's done well with his plumbing business. He has three employees and his own little storefront and he's gotten to where he doesn't have to work all the time now. He can enjoy life a little. The comics and the movie merch, they're his passion and he actually does make money from trading and selling all that stuff. He owned a copy of the very first *Captain America* comic book that *his* dad bought when it first came out."

All Wes could say to that was, "Wow."

Evy's cheeks had flushed deep red. "That comic book was precious to my dad. And now he's gone and sold it so he can give me even more than he has already. It's not right."

Wes had loved that light in her eyes when she'd talked about that shop of hers. And she really did seem ready to go with it. He had faith in her already. He believed that all she needed was the money to make it happen. "Evy, it does sound to me like you know what you're doing with your plans for your store. I can't help but admire your dad for wanting to back you. And from what you've said of Owen and what I've seen of the man, he's no fool. I think he sees your store as a damn good investment."

"Yeah, well. Two banks right here in town would beg to differ."

"Banks are conservative by definition. They will turn down a great proposal because there's a tiny element of risk."

"And so you think that I should let my dad take the risk?"

He thought that she needed backing and apparently her dad could afford to provide it. But Wes didn't say that. He could see from the fire in her eyes and the stubborn set of her strong chin that she wasn't ready to hear his opinion yet. She needed the right incentive—something to tempt her to get out of her own way and allow her dad to help her.

"I think I'm pushing too hard," he said mildly. "And that I've said enough. It's between you and your dad." He picked up the half-full wine bottle. "More wine?"

Her scowl melted away and a smile tugged at the corners of that beautiful mouth. "I do like a man who knows when to back off."

She held out her glass and he poured.

Evy couldn't remember when she'd had such a good time with a guy.

Not that she'd had all that much experience with men. But she'd dated a little in high school and her first year of college, too. And then there was Chad.

But really, Chad had been—well, kind of self-absorbed. He wore his hair just so and he talked about his family's beach house in the Outer Banks—or the OBX, as he called the barrier islands off the North Carolina coast. He took her to nice restaurants and he hung out with the power crowd. She'd wanted to impress him. But *fun* was never a word she would have used to describe him or the time she'd spent with him.

Wes, though… He made her laugh and he made her think. And he honestly did seem interested to know about her—about what she wanted in her life, what mattered to her.

She really needed to watch herself with him. They'd spent half the day together at Happy Hearts and then hours lingering over dinner at DJ's Deluxe. Yet, near midnight, when he walked her to her door, she wished she could think of a reason to invite him in.

But the lights were off inside. Her dad and Lola would be sound asleep in their beds. Time to call it a night.

She also needed to remember that this thing between her and Wes wasn't going anywhere— because there *was* no "thing." They'd had a nice day together and she had enjoyed a night out for once. End of story.

She stopped on the wide welcome mat beneath the glow of the porch light and faced him. "Thank you, Wes. I had such a good time tonight."

He took off his hat and dropped it on the padded wooden bench next to the door. "So did I. The best." His voice was rough velvet—and the way he looked at her, so intently... As though he intended to memorize everything about her.

She opened her mouth to say good-night. But before she could form a single word, his lips were there, his breath warm, smelling of coffee and caramel from their dessert.

All thought fled her mind.

A long sigh escaped her as he deepened the kiss. Encircling her in his arms, he pulled her body close. She felt...wrapped up in him, surrounded by his warmth and strength in the most exciting way. His mouth played on hers, his tongue teasing at the seam where her lips met.

She opened with a sigh.

He smelled so good, like the woods, like green grass and healthy male. He was everything natural and right. His tongue touched hers, stroking. She pressed closer, lost in the loveliest way—to the feel of him against her, enveloping her.

Oh, she could get fixed on him so easily, could find herself wanting only to hold on tight and never let go.

But who was she kidding? She was a working single mom with important goals to fulfill and no room in her life for love and all that foolishness. Not now, anyway. Not for a long time to come.

She needed *not* to let herself get carried away here.

Bringing her hands up between them, she braced

her palms on his chest and exerted just enough pressure to break the kiss.

He stared down at her, his mouth swollen, his eyes twin blue flames as he laid his big hand on her cheek. Her skin felt on fire.

How did he generate all this heat? She pressed her palms more firmly against his snow-white pearl snap shirt and tried to think of the right words to say. "We really shouldn't get anything started, Wes."

"Evy…" He said her name reproachfully.

His tone stiffened her spine. "What?"

"It's already started," he said in a low, rough rumble.

And then he was kissing her again.

She couldn't help herself, couldn't stop herself. She swayed toward him, needing to get closer, offering her mouth to him, longing for more.

It felt so good, his lips claiming hers, his arms banded nice and tight around her. It felt wonderful. Just right—even though she knew it was all wrong, that she shouldn't be letting herself feel swept away by him. It was only one evening, a great time with a good guy. Nothing more.

Not to mention, they were standing on her dad's front porch right under the light for all the neighbors to see.

Before she could collect her scattered wits and

step away, he broke the kiss. Again, her own yearning betrayed her. She had to fight the need to wrap her hands around the back of his head and yank that mouth of his down to hers once more.

Trouble. This man was trouble and she didn't need any of that. "I, uh…" Once again, her brain had gone offline. It did that way too much around him.

That smile of his. It truly could melt a girl's panties right off her body. "You were saying?"

"I really don't know. I seem to have lost my train of thought completely."

"I get it. I do."

"Somehow, I doubt that."

"Evy, sometimes around you, I can only stand there, staring, with no clue of what it was I meant to say. That's not like me at all. I'm the good-time guy, remember? I take things easy, no pressure, just fun. And as for what you said a minute ago, about not getting anything started… I get that. I'm no more ready for love than you are."

"Then what are we doing here?"

He traced a finger down the side of her throat, stirring goose bumps as he went. "Didn't we already talk this through?"

"You mean, about how it will be just for fun?"

"Yes."

"Just between…friends?"

"That's right."

"But someone could get hurt, Wes." And she had a very strong feeling that someone would be her. "People get expectations no matter how hard they promise themselves that they won't."

"Not necessarily. It's completely possible that two people could choose to live right now, in the moment. Not everything has to have a goal. Not every trip has a set destination. Sometimes you need to just climb on your horse or get in that pickup and ride."

"I'm a goal-oriented person. I always have been." She searched his eyes. "However…"

He skated slow hands up over her shoulders and then back down along her arms. Those unhurried twin caresses caused a warm little quiver all through her body. "Keep talking."

"Well, I do like you. And I can't help but wonder if maybe it's time I tried something a little bit different…"

He bent closer and brushed the sweetest, lightest kiss on the tip of her nose. "Something like what?"

"Like what you said. Something that's just for fun, just, you know, between friends."

He looked so serious suddenly. "*Maybe*, you said—meaning you're not sure?"

"No, Wes. I'm not sure. Tempted, yes. But not sure."

"So I need to give you a little time to think some more about it." And then he grinned that slow grin of his. "But not too long. In fact, tell you what. Next time, we can talk it over some more, we can talk all you want. We can get down in the weeds over it—should we or shouldn't we? Is it wrong or is it right? How much fun can we have before it all goes to hell?"

She groaned. "You are not reassuring me."

"Maybe not. But I like you, too. I like everything about you. I like that you're kind and I like that you're honest." He scooped up his hat from the bench cushion and settled it on his head. "And it sure doesn't hurt that you are so damn beautiful." He started walking backward down the steps, hands stuffed in his pockets, his gaze locked on hers. "I like your daughter and I like your dad. I want to know you better." He was halfway down the walk by then.

"Good night, Wes."

"'Night." He started to turn, but then he faced her again. "One more thing."

"Yeah?"

"You haven't seen the last of me. As long as you don't give me a flat-out no, Evy Roberts, I am going to be around."

Chapter Five

Back at the ranch, Wes considered getting Archie from Tyler and Callie, but he hesitated to bother them so late.

Yet somehow, when he reached the dirt road that led to Tyler's house, he took the turn anyway, just in case one of them might still be up. As he bumped along the rough road, his mind was filled with thoughts of Everlee. He'd just left her and already he missed the taste of her mouth, the way her body felt, soft in all the right places, pressed close to his.

He shouldn't want her so much. Wanting led to caring more than he should. And caring too much put his heart on the line. The whole idea was never to risk his heart again. And he really ought to give her a little space. She was reluctant to explore the attraction between them. He ought to respect her hesitation about spending too much time with him. He ought to back off.

But he knew he couldn't stay away from her. Tomorrow night, he would end up manufacturing one excuse or another to drive to Bronco Valley and drop in at Doug's for a beer.

When he rounded the last bend in the road to Tyler's house, he saw the light in the front window. Ty appeared on the porch with Archie just as Wes pulled the pickup to a stop.

He got out and ran up the steps. "Thanks for looking after him."

"No problem. I mean that. Archie here is a great guy." Tyler handed over the leash. The pup gave a happy little whine, those ears of his flopping as he looked back and forth between Wes and his brother. "Bring him by any time."

"Thanks again, Ty. Give my favorite niece a kiss for me?"

"You got it. You have a nice time with Evy?"

Wes had zero desire to discuss Evy with anyone—especially one of his nosy brothers. "Real nice, yeah."

"I think you like that girl."

"Yes, I do. I'll let you go. Come on, Archie."

"How about little Lola?" Ty called out as Wes went down the steps to his pickup. "You like her, too?"

"Oh, yeah. Lola is every bit as special as her mom," he replied as he pulled open the passenger-side door. Archie jumped in all by himself and settled right down on the seat.

"I think you're a goner," Ty said more softly.

Wes heard him clearly, though—and pretended he didn't. He waved without turning.

A few minutes later, he pulled in at the home-steader's cabin that had stood on Flying A land for more than a century.

His parents and his brothers had helped him fix up the cabin just this past spring when he'd decided he was done being the only one in the family to live in town. The ranch and the family business, Abernathy Meats, made them all a good living, and Wes knew how to manage his money. He invested wisely and he could live anywhere he chose.

After college—and the mess with Belinda—he'd wanted to get away from the family, to have his own place in town. In town he could party all night if he wanted to, have a pretty woman over and not get the third degree from his mom or one of his nosy brothers the next day.

But he was a rancher to the core. He loved getting out on the land. Driving back and forth from town every day to work cattle, mend fences and spread feed when it snowed had gotten old. Winters were the worst. Blizzards, deep snow and icy roads had meant he'd ended up just staying on the Flying A when the roads were bad. His condo in town sat empty while he slept in his childhood bedroom for weeks at a time.

The cabin worked well for him. Now he had his own space close to his work. Archie seemed to like the cabin, too. That night, he slept in his new dog bed in the corner of Wes's bedroom.

The next morning, he and Crosby rode out to check on some heifers in a far pasture. Wes brought Archie along. The dog was a natural, obedient and attentive.

Crosby liked him as much as Tyler did. "How's that pup doing with house-training?"

"Hasn't had an accident yet."

"Impressive."

"He's a good dog, all right."

"Tell you what, Wes. If that pup's too much for you, I would consider taking him off your hands."

Weston cast his youngest brother a cool glance. "No, thanks. Archie and I have an understanding. We're a team and that's not going to change."

That evening, Wes and Archie had dinner at Dean and Susanna's house. When Susanna opened the door, her puppy, Holly, eased out around her and headed straight for Archie. Both dogs wriggled and whined and sniffed each other in greeting— no surprise, really. After all, they were littermates.

Last December, Archie's wandering mother, Maggie, about to go into labor, had somehow found her way to the Bronco Theater Company, where Susanna and Dean were stuck waiting out a blizzard. Maggie had given birth right there in the theater that night, with Susanna and Dean standing by as each pup was born. Later, when the pups went up for adoption, Susanna had claimed Holly.

"A reunion," said Susanna fondly as she watched the two dogs greet each other. "It's so sweet to see them together. Come on in." She stepped back and pulled the door wider, clicking her tongue for Holly. Archie's sister gave her brother one last sniff and went inside. Wes and Archie followed her.

After dinner, Wes hung out with Dean for a while. They sat on the front porch with the dogs, who rolled around at their feet wrestling together, fake-growling at each other like the frisky pups they still were.

All that day, Wes had argued with himself about whether or not he ought to show up at Doug's tonight. In the end, he'd decided not to drive into town, after all.

Because he took Evy seriously. He thought the world of her. He wanted to be *friends* with her—

friends with benefits eventually, he hoped—but friends, first and foremost.

If he just *had* to see her every chance he got, well, she might consider that taking things too far. Might call it *more* than friendship. So tonight he would give them both a break from his pursuit of her, give her a little much-needed space.

"You got something on your mind?" Dean asked.

It was half past eight. Twilight had begun to change the color of the sky, turning the snow left on the peaks of the distant mountains the palest pink. From somewhere behind the house, an owl hooted.

"Wes?"

"Huh?" He frowned at his brother who watched him a little too closely from the other chair.

"Man, you are a million miles away."

Archie rolled close to Wes's chair. He reached down and gave the mutt a scratch behind the ear. "Just thinking…"

"About?"

Green eyes and a waterfall of black hair. "Nothin' much." He stood and stretched.

What was she doing about now?

He smiled to himself as he pictured her, all that beautiful hair pinned up, in her crisp white shirt and snug jeans, flitting from one table of noisy cowboys to the next, never stopping for long, making sure that every customer got their order fast and just the way they liked it. "You know, I think I'll head on into town, get a beer. How 'bout you?"

"We've got beer in the fridge, Weston."

"Come on. We'll go to Doug's. Let's see if Susanna wants to come, too."

"No, thanks. I'm an almost-married man now. When you live with the right woman, you find you kind of like staying home."

"Suit yourself."

"Oh, I intend to—and why don't you leave Archie here with us? I'll take him over to your place before we go to bed."

Wes looked down at his dog. Archie worked so hard to please that sometimes Wes forgot he was only six months old. "That'd be great. He's still a pup, and it's only his second night on the Flying A. Don't want to leave him alone for too long."

"He can stay with us anytime. I can already tell he's an easy guy to look after, just like his sister."

"'Preciate that."

Wes went in and thanked Susanna for the meal. When he came back out, Archie got up to go with him. He bent to give the dog a pat on the head. When he rose, Archie stared up at him expectantly.

"Stay," he said.

The pup dropped to his haunches with a worried whine. Funny how dogs sometimes seemed human. Archie had been left behind and he didn't want that happening to him again. "Stay for a while with Holly," Wes said, knowing he was using way more words than Archie would understand, but hoping the eye contact and reassuring tone would soothe him. "Dean will bring you home later."

Archie gave another worried whine, but he didn't try to follow when Wes left.

Evy's shift at Doug's began at eight. She entered the bar to find that Doug had already replaced the broken window by the Death Stool. Everything was back to normal, as though that rock had never come flying right at her and ended up whacking Wes on the shoulder.

Compared to Saturday night, Wednesday was a snooze fest. It had been this way last year, too, people taking a break from partying after four days of Red, White and Bronco.

Evy kept busy. When she had a spare moment, she tackled her side work. That way at closing time, she could head right on home. Doug might even let her go at midnight. He could handle the place by himself when it got slow.

Tips were scarce on a night like tonight. She had most of her side work done in the first hour. After that, time dragged and her mind started wandering to places she probably shouldn't let it go.

She kept thinking about Wes, wondering what

he was up to, picturing him hanging out with Archie and his brothers at the Flying A. Really, she had no expectation that she might see him tonight and it annoyed her to no end that she felt kind of melancholy about that.

Please. She and Weston had hung out together. He'd been nice to her little girl. She'd gone to dinner with him. Once. This was not deathless love.

It was casual. Just friends. Oh, and he was a really good kisser. End of story. Period. Full stop. A little distance was a very good thing. It wasn't as if they were in a relationship, after all. That was the last thing she'd ever be getting into right now.

She'd just convinced herself that she didn't expect him tonight and she wouldn't be seeing him and that was fine with her when he walked in the door.

A plate of nachos in one hand and a full pitcher in the other, she just happened to be looking that way when he entered. His gaze locked right on her and he tipped his hat with a slow, sexy smile.

"Earth to Evy," said Malone, a grizzled old cowboy who'd been the cook at the Ambling A Ranch for as long as anyone in town could remember. Abernathys—yet another branch of the powerful family—owned the Ambling A. "Just set those nachos and that pitcher right down here, pretty lady," Malone instructed.

Evy blasted him with her brightest smile and put his order on the table in front of him. "Enjoy." She filled his glass.

Malone winked at her. "Thank you, I sure will."

When she got back to the bar, Wes was sitting right there next to the haunted stool. Doug had already served him a beer.

The night seemed so much brighter, more alive, more interesting, now that *he* was here.

Should that alarm her?

Probably.

But right at this moment, she felt light as a moonbeam. She floated on air. "You think maybe you're taking a chance, sitting right beside the Death Seat?" she teased.

Wes took a slow sip of beer. "I like to live dangerously."

She clucked her tongue at him as Doug stepped close on the other side of the bar and asked, "What do you need, Everlee?"

She gave him her order. As he filled it, she tried not to stare at Wes with a big silly grin on her face. Had he come to see her? The very idea thrilled her all out of proportion.

For the next two hours, she tried her best to keep her mind on her work and not let herself wander too close to the tall, handsome cowboy who lingered at the bar. He never once in all that time tried to strike up a conversation with her.

She started thinking that she must have gotten it wrong. He hadn't come to see her, after all. She decided she would *not* allow herself to feel let down when he left.

Oh, but he stayed. And the longer he stayed, the more her anticipation built all over again. She began letting herself sneak a peek at him now and then. Half the time, he was looking at her when she glanced his way.

At midnight, Doug said, "Everlee honey, it's deader than a hammer in here. And I see you're all caught up on your side work. You cash in. Go home and get some sleep. I'll close up on my own."

"Thanks, Doug."

She traded in her meager tips for a couple of larger bills, dashed back to the breakroom, washed her hands, took off her apron and put it in her locker. Feeling hyped up and more than a little bit foolish, she brushed out her hair and put on some lip gloss. Finally, hooking her bag over her shoulder, she marched out to the bar again—to find the seat by the haunted stool empty.

Her heart sank.

But then Doug said, "That Abernathy boy is waiting for you outside. Don't go breaking his heart now, you hear?"

She leaned across the bar and kissed Doug on the cheek. "I would never."

He grinned at her. "'Night."

"'Night."

Outside, the half-moon hung over the Big Snowy Mountains and the stars looked close enough to reach up and touch. Wes leaned against his crew cab several feet away.

"Evy." He said her name low, yet the sound seemed to echo in the air around her. It was so quiet out, just a lone frog croaking somewhere in the bushes at the edge of the parking lot and a single car passing on the deserted street nearby.

She went to him. He straightened from his easy slouch against the vehicle as she approached, halting when her work shoes were inches from his boots. He took off his hat.

"I kept thinking you would leave," she said, her voice oddly breathless.

"I kept telling myself I should."

"But you didn't."

"I don't see that little Outback of yours."

"It's not that far to the house and it's a nice night out."

"I don't know, Evy. Walking home after midnight? That can't be safe."

"Stop. It's Bronco. Safest town in the USA."

"I might have agreed with you—until that rock came flying through the window last week."

Her heart stuttered in her chest. "Are you saying you think someone was actually trying to hurt *me*, in particular?"

"No." He clasped her shoulder, a steadying touch. "That's not what I meant." His teasing look had vanished to be replaced by real concern. "I don't believe anyone is trying to hurt you, specifically. Honestly, who knows what whoever threw that rock might have been thinking? But judging by the note wrapped around it, I think we can safely say that you weren't the target. You just happened to be standing in the way. Anyway, what I meant to say is, why not be safe and ride home with me?"

"What did I just tell you? Bronco *is* safe. Even in the middle of the night."

That devilish half smile curved one corner of his mouth again. "So ride home with me, anyway."

"Honestly. Do you ever give up?"

"Never." He bent his head slowly, giving her time to back away.

But she didn't.

They shared a quick, sweet kiss. Her heart lifted and the night seemed full of promise. She felt young again, carefree. How long had it been since she'd felt this way?

Too long.

"Come on. Get in my truck."

"So bossy." She laughed and stepped back so he could pull open the driver's-side door. She clambered up behind the wheel and scrambled over the console, giggling like a teenager as she went.

He was right behind her, sliding into his seat, shutting the door and tossing his hat back over his shoulder. "Okay now. Where were we?"

"Right about…here." She leaned in.

He met her halfway, his lips so warm, his outdoorsy scent surrounding her. Her giggles quickly became soft sighs as the kiss grew hot and deep. He wrapped those hard arms around her and she moaned.

It felt so good, kissing Wes. It felt right, somehow. As though she'd been waiting all her life to kiss him.

"This damn console," he grumbled against her parted lips.

"Shh…" She kissed him some more.

"We should get in back."

Talk about tempting. She retreated just far enough to press a finger against those beautiful lips of his. "Uh-uh. Too dangerous."

He groaned, but he didn't argue. They kissed some more, long, deep, drugging kisses. She never wanted to stop.

However, reality would not be denied. "Wes, I

really have to go home." She tried to retreat to her side of the cab.

But he commanded, "Get back here." She couldn't resist and met him halfway. He kissed her one more time, instructing, "Buckle up," when she sat back in her seat again.

A few minutes later, he pulled in at the foot of the sloping front walk that led to her front door.

"Thank you for the ride," she said softly. *And for all those perfect kisses, too.*

"I'll walk you to the door."

"Uh-uh. We'll just start kissing again."

He held her in her seat by the force of that blue gaze alone. "Let me take you and Lola out to the ranch. Just for a few hours. I'll have you back in plenty of time for work. Pick you up at noon?"

The thing was, she really wanted to say yes. "Today?"

He nodded. "Come on. It'll be fun. Lola will love it."

"You're way too convincing."

He leaned toward her again. And somehow, she found herself leaning in, too. "All right, then." His mouth brushed hers, both tender and arousing. "I'll be here at noon."

"I'll pack a picnic lunch."

"No need. I'll take care of lunch."

She thought of Chad then, always taking control,

rarely letting her contribute. Because he had the money and nothing she could provide would compare with what he had to offer, so why shouldn't he do it all? "I like to do my part, Wes. I'll bring the lunch."

He studied her face for a moment. "All right. You bring lunch."

Nine hours later, during breakfast, Evy told her daughter that Weston had invited them to the ranch for the day.

Lola jumped up and down. "Mommy, I want to wear my red jeans with my purple belt and pink boots and my green shirt with the diamonds on the collar." They were actually rhinestones, but why quibble? Lola loved that shirt.

"You would look beautiful in that."

"I know, Mommy." Her smile was sweet and modest.

Evy explained that Lola's best outfits should be saved for other trips. Lola frowned at that news. In the end, though, she let Evy guide her and wore everyday jeans, a T-shirt and her plain brown boots. She brought along her straw cowboy hat with the chin strap, too.

She also begged to bring Valentina, but Evy held firm that Tina would stay home.

Wes had Archie with him when he came to pick them up.

Lola loved that the pup sat in the back seat of the crew cab with her. She talked nonstop through the ride to the Flying A, mostly about petting cows and the picnic she'd helped Evy pack.

Wes assured her she would see plenty of cows. "But as a rule, we don't pet them," he cautioned.

At the ranch, he drove straight to the horse barn where one of the hands had tacked up a small chestnut mare named Babycakes. Delighted, Lola put on her hat and Wes hoisted her into the child-sized saddle. She beamed with pride and excitement as he patiently led the mare in slow circles around the paddock while Evy and Archie watched from the other side of the fence.

Next, Wes gave them a tour of his cabin. It was rustic, but comfortable, with stone pillars supporting the deep front porch and two dormer windows upstairs. The kitchen and living area took up most of the downstairs, with his bedroom and a bathroom in back. Upstairs, it was one big open space.

"Big enough for two bedrooms and another bathroom," he explained. "I'll get to that this winter, I hope. Maybe later I'll add on to the main structure."

Lola stood in front of the stone fireplace in the middle of the living area and turned in a circle, arms outstretched and her head tipped back, a giant smile on her face. "I like it so much, Weston. It's a real cowboy house."

He laughed and agreed that it was.

Dean's fiancée, Susanna, joined them for lunch at the picnic table under a tall hickory tree not far from the cabin. She brought Archie's littermate Holly with her.

Evy had always liked Susanna, who was kindhearted and a lot of fun. Now she seemed truly happy, too—with Dean and with their life together.

Maybe someday, Evy thought, feeling suddenly wistful—only to quickly remind herself that she had a daughter to raise and a business dream to fulfill before she would let herself even consider getting too serious with some guy.

She really shouldn't have glanced in Wes's direction right then, but then she did it anyway. He was watching her, a speculative gleam in his eyes. She flashed him a bright smile and sipped from her tall glass of lemonade.

As for Lola, she nibbled chips and ate half her sandwich, sneaking the rest of it to the puppies. She picked wildflowers and presented a half-crushed handful of them to Evy. "For you, Mommy."

Evy kissed her velvety cheek and whispered, "I love them, Lolly. Thank you."

Too soon, it was time to climb back in the pickup and head for town. At the house on Union Street,

Wes left Archie in the pickup and helped carry the picnic stuff inside. Lola insisted he say hi to Tina, which he did, taking the kitten in those fine, big hands of his, nuzzling her furry cheek.

When he handed her back to Lola, she thanked him without having to be prompted. "It was the best day ever, Weston. I can't wait till we can do it again. Tell Babycakes I miss her a lot."

"Will do," Wes replied.

Evy walked him to the door.

"I miss *you*," he whispered as she ushered him out.

She stepped out and pulled the door shut behind her. "How can you miss me? I'm right here."

He actually pouted. "Yeah. But not for long." He bent close and stole a quick kiss. "See you soon." And then he turned and headed off down the front walk.

See you soon…

She liked the sound of that far too much. She also spent the first half of her shift at Doug's that night anticipating his arrival. When he failed to appear, her spirits sagged at the same time as she reminded herself not to be ridiculous.

Why should she feel let down? She'd seen him just that afternoon.

Then her foolish heart skipped more than one

beat when she checked her phone during her break and found a text from him.

I'm up before dawn tomorrow morning. Fences to mend. Ditches to burn. Archie and I will be busy. Guess I better turn in early. Thinking of you...

She almost texted back. But if he slept with his phone by the bed, a text alert might wake him. She put her phone away—and for the rest of her shift, her steps felt lighter and so did her heart.

She waited to reply to his text until the next morning when she got up at ten. But by then, well, she didn't know what to say. *Thinking of you, too?*

Miss you?

Uh-uh. Anything she might say would come across as either sappy or silly—or like, maybe she cared for him a lot more than she should. Like maybe she ached to get to know him better, to spend every spare moment at his side until he'd shared all the secrets of his heart and she'd done the same.

Until he was hers and she was his and—

No. Just no.

She couldn't get anything started with him. Her life was jam-packed already with zero room for romance.

As she set her phone back on the nightstand and

went to get dressed, she knew she'd made the right decision. Except in a casual, no-strings way, she and Wes Abernathy were not meant to be.

Chapter Six

"Lie-berry day!" announced Lola when Evy joined her daughter and her dad in the kitchen. "Eat your breakfast, Mommy, and let's go!"

Forty-five minutes later, the two of them entered the Bronco Library, a grand structure in the heart of the Bronco Heights business and shopping district. Lola knew the drill. She dropped off her books at reception and headed straight for Shari Lormand's desk in the middle of the children's section.

Shari, the children's librarian, had curly strawberry blond hair. She wore the cutest tortoiseshell glasses and usually had a mischievous gleam in her eyes.

She greeted them with a bright smile. "Good morning, Lola," she said in a hushed voice. "Evy, hello."

"Hi there," Evy whispered back. She thought the world of Shari. They'd met when Evy started bringing Lola to Shari's weekly story time, and quickly become friends.

Lola practiced her library voice, too—though it was more of a whisper-shout. "Hi, Miss Shari! I turned in my books and I need some new ones!"

"You've been reading." Shari nodded in approval.

"Oh, yes, I have." Lola mostly memorized the books when Shari, Evy or Pop-Pop read them aloud to her. But already, she recognized a lot of words when she saw them on the page.

"Story time in half an hour," said Shari.

"I can't wait!" Lola trotted right over to join her friends and a few parents, leaving Shari and Evy alone.

"You've got a look," whispered Shari.

"I don't know what you're talking about."

"Yes, you do. You've got stars in your eyes." Evy's friend was much too perceptive. Shari had a gift for understanding human relationships. She truly cared about people and about what made them tick.

Evy took the chair beside her friend's desk and leaned close. "I shouldn't say anything…"

"Tell me," Shari commanded.

Evy glanced around the bright, open space. For the moment at least, they were alone. "Okay, there's a guy."

Shari's eyes widened behind the lenses of her glasses. "Excellent."

"Please. You know very well I've got no time for a guy."

Shari waved a hand, as though batting off an annoying fly. "And *you* know I'm going to need a name."

"I shouldn't tell you."

"Tell me anyway. Now. Before someone interrupts us."

"Oh, fine," Evy grumbled. "It's Weston Abernathy."

"Ah. The one who rescued you from the curse of Doug's famous Death Seat."

Evy stifled a groan. "You heard about that?"

"I think everybody in town has heard about that by now. Did they ever find out who threw the rock?"

"As far as I know it's still a mystery."

Shari braced her elbow on her desk and propped her chin on her hand. "Weston Abernathy, huh? That one's a charmer."

"Too charming if you ask me."

Eyes twinkling, Shari leaned closer. "You *really* like him."

"I did not say that."

"Please. As if you *had* to say it."

"Okay, fine. I think I'm falling for him." The whispered words were out of her mouth before Evy could stop them. She slapped her forehead with her own hand. "Oh, Shari. I know better. I really do. But he's not only hot, he's thoughtful. He's kind. Lola adores him. That man is…well, he's pretty much impossible to resist."

"So don't resist. Go for it. Love is hard to find, Evy."

"I never exactly said it was love."

"You didn't exactly have to say it."

"No, really, I mean it. I've been hyper aware of him for a long time. For nearly a year, really. But I've barely even spoken to him until the incident with the rock last week. Since then, yes, we have spent some time together. I've gotten to know him, a little. The attraction is so strong. But I'm trying to keep a lid on it. Trying just to be friends."

Shari wasn't fooled. "Friends. Right."

"Come on, Shari. Don't look at me like that."

Shari grinned and slowly nodded her head. "I mean it. You need to go for it."

"You said that already."

"And it bears repeating. Love is rare and precious. And it's downright wrong to throw it away when it finally comes knocking."

After a nine-hour day of burning ditches and mending fences, Wes took a long, hot shower. He put on dress jeans and a nice shirt, dropped Archie off with Susanna and drove into town, where he paid a visit to Carlson's Commercial Properties.

The office was just closing for the weekend, but he managed to get a few minutes with a broker he knew. Wes explained what he was looking for and the broker, whose name was Glen Dobson, said he had nothing right then, but he promised to give Wes a call if anything that fit his specifications became available.

To firm up the connection with good old Glen, Wes suggested dinner. They went to DJ's Deluxe, where Wes plied the broker with good Scotch and great steak.

When they parted outside the restaurant at a little after nine, Glen said, "Tell you what. I'll make a few calls. I might have something good for you on Monday. Call me first thing. I'm in the office at eight sharp."

"Will do." They shook hands and parted ways.

Wes's plan was to head back to the ranch, pick up his dog from Susanna and get a good night's sleep.

He hadn't seen or even spoken to Evy since they'd said goodbye on her doorstep yesterday afternoon.

Which was fine. Good.

He fully intended to let the whole weekend pass before seeking her out again. Yeah, he wanted to be with her—he wanted that a lot. But he had to be careful here. They'd agreed this wasn't going anywhere too serious.

As her friend, he wanted to help her achieve her dreams, to make her life a little better in any way he could.

But if he showed up to see her every single chance he got, well, that would mean he'd let this thing with her get out of control—and he was Wes Abernathy. He didn't do serious and he never got out of control.

He probably shouldn't even have sent her that text last night—the one she didn't answer.

Yeah. He needed to pick up his dog and go home.

And yet somehow, ten minutes later, he found himself pulling into the parking lot at Doug's.

Evy spotted Wes as he walked in the door—probably because she'd been keeping an eye on that door since her shift started. Foolishly, she'd hoped that he might show up.

He looked so handsome in a dark blue shirt, good jeans and high-dollar boots, the lights overhead picking up hints of auburn in his deep brown hair. Of course, he saw her staring. A smile spread across his face.

She'd just loaded up a trayful of drinks for a table near the dance floor. At the sight of him, she stopped stock-still a few feet from the bar.

He came right to her, his long strides eating up the distance between them. "Hey." He tipped his cream-colored hat to her.

"Wes."

"Good to see you."

"Yes."

They stared at each other, both of them grinning—until some cowboy shouted, "Evy! We need those drinks over here!"

That got them both moving. He took a seat at the bar and she went back to work.

After that, the night just seemed to fly by. Wes stayed. He won at 8-ball, sat at the bar off and on and visited with Hattie Hawkins, who'd dropped by to say hi to Doug.

The crowd started thinning out around one. At two, when Doug closed the doors, Weston was the only customer left in the place. Usually, Doug shooed everyone out at closing time, but he didn't say a word to Wes about leaving.

"I'll be outside," her favorite cowboy said softly as she was wiping down the bar.

She sent him a secret smile, just between the two of them. "I won't be long."

And she wasn't. They ended up in his crew cab, steaming up the windows, kissing across the front-seat console like a couple of teenagers. He really did make her feel younger, somehow. Like the world was all new again, the future bright before her. Like anything was possible.

Including love and happiness with the one man meant for her—not that she was in any way ready for any such thing. But still. It did feel so good. To have his strong arms around her and his lips on hers, coaxing her to open and let him in.

After they'd shared so many kisses that her lips felt swollen and deliciously sore, he drove her home.

Saturday night was pretty much a repeat. He showed up at nine and stayed until closing. They smooched in the parking lot. He drove her home again, walked her to the door and kissed her some more.

Before they said good-night, she agreed to spend the afternoon with him at the ranch tomorrow. "I'll pick you and Lola up at noon. She can go riding, same as last time. And since you're off tomorrow night, I'd love for you to stay for dinner. Abernathy Meats have the best steaks in the county. I've got serious grilling skills and I aim to impress you."

The next morning, Lola insisted on bringing

the stack of children's books she'd checked out at the library the day before. "Miss Shari says it's always good to bring some books wherever you go, Mommy. Then if you have to take a little rest or you just want a piece of quiet, you will have something good to read."

"A *piece* of quiet, huh?"

Lola wrinkled her nose with a frown. "Did I say it wrong?"

"No, honey. I think you said it exactly right."

At the ranch, Lola got to ride her "favorite horse in the whole world." She played with Archie and Holly. Later in the afternoon, Callie and Tyler brought Maeve over and Lola decided to "read" to her from one of her library books, reciting the words and even some short passages she'd memorized when Shari read them at story time—and filling in the blanks with her own vivid imagination. Maeve was enthralled.

For dinner, served at the picnic table under the hickory tree, they had juicy T-bones, baked potatoes with all the fixings, corn on the cob and a big green salad. Lola ate everything on her plate and polished off a slice of apple pie baked by Wes's mom, Hannah.

After the pie, Lola asked to lie down. "Just to rest."

Minutes after she stretched out on the big leather sofa in the cabin, she was sound asleep. Evy covered her with a soft old afghan Wes's grandmother had made.

Then Wes took Evy's hand and led her out to the front porch. They sat side by side in a pair of Adirondack chairs, watching the sunset. It was almost ten when she said she really needed to get back to town.

At the Union Street house, Wes carried the sleeping Lola inside. Evy led the way to Lola's room, where she pulled back the covers and Wes laid Lola gently down. She'd already taken off her boots—hours ago, when she'd stretched out on the cabin's sofa to read. Evy didn't want to wake her, so she left her in her jeans and T-shirt, tucking her Disney Princess comforter gently around her.

Out in the hallway, Wes whispered, "No sign of your dad. Guess he's sound asleep by now, huh?"

She glanced down at her dad's shut door. "I'm pretty sure he's gone to Dotty's house for the night. They've been together for a few years now. They really like each other."

Wes cradled her face between his big warm hands. His eyes gleamed at her through the shadows. "I really like *you*."

"Show me." She went on tiptoe.

They stood there in the dim hallway for several minutes, kissing slow and deep.

Finally, she made herself step back.

He touched the side of her face, caught a lock of her hair, wound it around a finger and then let it loose. "I should go, huh?"

Did she want him to leave?

No.

But she wasn't quite ready to take that next step. She grabbed his hand and led him to the front door, stepping outside with him for one last kiss.

"See you soon," he said. "Real soon, I hope."

She peered up at him more closely. "You've got a funny look, like you know something I don't. Is something going on?"

"Not a thing. Good night." He saluted her with a tip of his hat and then went on down the steps to his truck.

"Everlee…" It was her dad's voice, followed by the sound of knuckles tapping on her bedroom door.

With a groan, she fought her way up from deep sleep. Fumbling for her phone, she grabbed it off the nightstand. "Nine in the morning?" she muttered softly to herself and then groaned. Nine was too early for a girl who worked nights. Her dad understood that. As a rule, even on her days off, she tried to be up by ten. But nine was pushing it. "Ugh. What the…?"

Owen knocked again. "Honey, you awake?"

"I am now," she grumbled to herself. "Coming!"

Tossing back the covers, she padded barefoot to the door and stuck her head out. Her dad blinked at the sight of her. His mouth twisted like he was trying not to laugh.

"What?" she demanded. "Everything okay?"

"Weston's here."

"He is?"

"He needs to talk to you."

"About what?"

"You'll have to ask him."

She blinked and covered a yawn, then glanced down at her wrinkled sleep shirt and shorts. "Give him coffee."

"I already did."

"Thanks. I'll put some clothes on and be there in a few minutes." She could hear Lola chattering away out in the kitchen. "I'm guessing Lolly's keeping him entertained."

"You'd better believe it."

In the bathroom, Evy discovered that a big clump of her hair was tangled on top of her head, a rat's nest poking almost straight up. No wonder her dad had been trying not to laugh.

Fifteen minutes later, she'd rinsed her face, brushed her teeth, more or less tamed her hair and pulled on some jeans and a tank top.

She joined the others in the kitchen. Pausing to plant a kiss on Lola's dark head and give her dad a side hug in his chair at the table, she filled her favorite mug with coffee and didn't move from the counter until she'd taken more than one heavenly sip.

"Sleep well?" asked Weston.

"I *was*, yes." She tried to look grumpy but knew that she didn't succeed. Wes could show up at six in the morning for all she cared. She would still be glad to see him—and did he have to be so handsome? It just wasn't fair that the guy should look so good, especially so early in the morning.

Lola leaned toward him and whispered loudly, "Mommy can be cranky when she gets up."

"I see," he said, nodding at Lola and then shifting his gaze back to Evy. "You look fresh as a daisy to me."

She scoffed—but then remembered her manners. "Thank you. What's up?"

"I was wondering if you would go for a ride with me."

"I'll go!" Lola sang out.

Her dad rose. "Lollipop, let's go see Dotty."

"Right now, Pop-Pop?"

"There might be waffles in it for you. With whip cream and strawberries."

Three minutes later, Owen and Lola were out the front door.

Evy poured herself more coffee and filled Wes's cup, too. "I'm having toast. You want some?"

"I would love some toast."

She fixed the toast, slathering it liberally with butter, setting out two kinds of jam. "Okay, what's going on?" she demanded as she moved Lola's booster to the next seat over and took the chair beside him.

"I want you to see a storefront on Commercial Street, right in the heart of Valley Center. The style is rustic industrial chic—big windows, exposed ductwork, high ceilings, aged brick."

She set down her toast without taking a bite. "Did you just say 'rustic industrial chic'?"

He shrugged. "That's what the broker I talked to called it. He showed me the storefront this morning. From what you've told me about Cimarron Rose, this might be the perfect location. It's not far from the park and it's surrounded by other shops that Glen—the broker—assures me are thriving. I believe him. At eight fifteen this morning, the coffee place across the street was full of customers. The retail shops looked interesting, well kept up and inviting. And of course, it's all verifiable before you make any kind of decision. It's not cheap, but I think you can talk him down a little or get better terms. After all, Valley Center is nice, but it's not Bronco Heights."

Her mind was now spinning. Furry warmth brushed her ankles. Bending, she picked up Tina and gave her a kiss between her pointy black ears before carefully setting the kitten back down.

Stalling, she sipped more coffee, almost choking on it because her throat felt so tight. She had no clue what to say. He'd just described her ideal retail location. Was this even real?

Maybe she was still sound asleep in her bed, having a lovely, impossible dream.

In a small voice, she asked, "Not far from Sadie's Holiday House, right?" The year-round Christmas gift shop was a big favorite with just about every kid on both sides of town—and most adults, too. Her mom used to take her there when she was little.

Wes gave her a slow grin. "As a matter of fact, Sadie's Holiday House is next door."

Her heart actually leaped. She felt it bounce against her rib cage—and then grow heavy as she reminded herself of reality. "Oh, Wes. I can't believe you went to all that trouble for me. But you know I'm not ready. The banks haven't been—"

"Evy. Your dad wants to help you. He believes in you and so do I."

"I told you. I can't—"

"Just come with me. Just have a look at it. Glen can meet us there at ten thirty."

"No, really. I'd be wasting your time *and* his time, and I—"

"Stop right there. No matter what you decide,

you are not wasting my time. And Glen Dobson is a broker. It's his job to show properties whether a deal gets made or not."

Oh, the way he looked at her. Like he just couldn't wait to make all her dreams come true. Every time she thought he couldn't be more wonderful he proved her wrong.

He took her hand. "Come on. Just have a look. The property only became available Friday. I know you're the expert. But I listened when you told me all about your store and I have a really good feeling about this property, that it's the place for Cimarron Rose. You need to move fast, though. It's a great location in a beautiful building. Someone is going to snap it right up."

She laughed then. "But no pressure, right?"

"Just have a look at it, okay? That's all I'm asking for."

An hour later, she was shaking Glen Dobson's hand.

The broker led her and Wes around the empty store, pointing out all the features—gorgeous hardwood floors, original to the building, a tired-looking restroom that she could easily spruce up with fresh paint and new fixtures. There was even a small kitchen in back, which she would definitely put to good use. For her grand opening and other sales events, she would be providing snacks and treats to serve her customers. She wanted to make them feel welcome and appreciated.

Best of all? Location, location, location. Bean & Biscotti, her favorite coffee place, was directly across the street, with Sadie's Holiday House right where Wes had promised it would be—next door. The shop on her other side sold quality men's Western wear. Commercial Street buzzed with activity.

She couldn't help but get carried away imagining how it might be, that she could get to know her fellow shopkeepers and join forces with them. They could plan promotions together, joint sales events that would boost the profiles of each of their shops—and of Valley Center as a whole.

On the downside, the lease was more than she'd budgeted for. But she hadn't taken three years of business classes at UNC for nothing. It was a gross lease, meaning the landlord would pay taxes, insurance, repairs and utilities, and Evy would lock in her costs.

Really, it wouldn't get any better than this and she knew it.

Her phone rang in her hand. It was her dad. She signaled Wes and Glen that she would take the call and stepped through the door that led to the storeroom.

"Well?" her dad asked.

Tears filled her eyes. She blinked them away. "Let me guess. Wes told you everything before you got me up this morning."

"He only said that he thought he'd found the perfect location for your store. Was he right?"

Carefully, she dashed a tear from each eye. "Oh, Dad…"

"That was a yes?"

"Yes."

"I thought so—and, sweetheart, your grandpa would be so proud to think that a comic book he bought in 1941 financed the opening of his granddaughter's first store."

A loud bray of laughter escaped her. Through the open doorway, she could see Wes and the broker turning her way, looking slightly startled. She mouthed an apology at them and said to her dad, "My *first* store?"

"Time will tell. But, honey, you've got the brains, the grit and the know-how. You will succeed at whatever you choose to do. Never sell yourself short."

"How could I ever sell myself short with you around?"

"Take it." His voice was rough with emotion. "You deserve it. And I'll get to say that I helped you get started, which is a lot more to brag about than my classic comics collection."

She fumbled in her shoulder bag for a tissue. "I love you, Dad. Thank you. Thank you more than I can ever say."

Chapter Seven

Evy already had a business bank account set up for Cimarron Rose. That account had just over four hundred dollars in it—or it did until her dad transferred a hundred and fifty thousand to it. By four that afternoon, the details had been hammered out, the lease signed, and Evy had the keys and the alarm code to her perfect Valley Center storefront.

Back at her house, as they went up the front walk hand in hand, Wes said, "We should celebrate— you, me, your dad, Lola and Dotty. I'm taking you all to dinner at The Association." The Association was the local cattleman's club and very exclusive. All the rich ranchers in Bronco had memberships.

She thought of Chad, always taking her to the fanciest places. There was nothing wrong with fancy. But she didn't want anything fancy tonight. Tonight, she wanted to celebrate her way—and on her own dime.

Evy teased, "Do they have Happy Meals there?"

"At The Association, they aim to please. I'm sure they'll have something that Lola would like."

"I have a better idea…" Instead of leading him inside, she pulled him to one end of the porch. "How about Bronco Burgers instead? It's casual. It's right here in Bronco Valley. The food is great and it will be my treat."

He stepped in closer and fiddled with the collar of the red jacket she'd put on that morning before they left to meet Glen Dobson on Commercial Street. "You never let me spoil you."

She leaned up and brushed her lips against his. "Oh, you spoil me plenty. We both know you do."

"Not as much as I want to." He growled the words and then kissed her again, deeper this time, until her toes curled in her favorite high-heeled turquoise boots tooled with twining red roses. She could feel his arousal pressed against her and she had that lovely, heavy sensation low down in her belly, the kind that made her think of getting him alone somewhere completely private, somewhere with a big bed close by.

When he lifted his head, Wes looked as breathless as she felt. "Okay, never mind The Association. Bronco Burgers it is."

"My treat."

"However you want it, Evy. That's how it will be."

Wes had a great time that evening. At Bronco Burgers they ordered giant burgers with endless fries. Many a tall glass of Pepsi was raised to the success of Cimarron Rose.

Later, after Lola was in bed and Owen and Dotty had gone across the street to her house, Wes followed Evy out the back door. She led him to the big oak in the center of the yard and pulled him down to a porch swing suspended from a thick branch.

"My dad built this swing," she said, her eyes a little misty. "He and my mom used to sit out here all the time. Sometimes I would sit with them. I used to feel so safe, tucked between them on this swing my dad had made, like nothing could hurt me, ever. I had everything a little girl could ever need." She leaned her head on his shoulder. "I was twelve when my mom died. It was so hard, without her. My dad was just lost for a long time. But the years went by. We made it through, you know?"

He wrapped his arm around her. "You're strong."

"Yes, I am." She looked up at him.

He lowered his head and they shared a long, sweet chain of kisses. Wes wished they could stay out here in the shadow of this big tree all night, with the stars and the moon way up there in the velvet sky, winking at them between the branches.

She talked about Lola. "She's strong and healthy now, but she was sick all the time as a baby. She had allergies to everything. She got every bug that came along. And ear infections, too. You name it, Lola got it. I had planned to go back to UNC to finish my degree, but for the first few years, being Lola's mom was a round-the-clock job. Getting my bachelor's just never happened."

He brushed a kiss against her temple. "You could still go back."

"I don't think so. That degree just isn't as important to me now. I always wanted to own my own shop. That was the goal." She beamed him a giant smile. "And now, with my dad's help and yours, I'll be living that dream."

Evy was something special, so proud and independent. Not to mention gorgeous and smart and smoking hot. She drove him wild, she really did. He'd never felt so taken by a woman—not even Belinda, really, though he'd worshipped Belinda with his whole heart and soul.

Admiration, though. That was a new thing for him. To want a woman so powerfully and to admire her, too. Evy had that ability to roll with the punches, to pick up the pieces and keep going whatever life dished out. He truly believed she could and would achieve any goal she set for herself. He even liked her stubborn pride, of all things. She always had to give back, to pay her share.

And tonight? Tonight she was on fire, lit up like a roman candle now that her dream for her future was starting to come true. The sweet scent of her tempted him. Her kisses really got him going—and then she would pull away and start in about her plans for her store.

He even loved listening to her go on about that. "I figure three months till my grand opening—late September, maybe. I need to choose a contractor to build the counters and displays, and to update the restroom and make a few crucial changes to the kitchen. I need a new fridge, a bigger sink and more counter space in there. I'm serving champagne and snacks for the opening. It all has to be just right…"

"So you'll be giving your notice at Doug's?"

"I'm going to talk to him about cutting my hours back. But if Doug agrees, I would like to keep on at the bar for a while yet. The money helps, I'm good at waiting tables and Doug is a friend—and so great to work for. We'll just see how it goes." She leaned her head on his shoulder.

He gathered her a little closer and almost wished

for things he knew he would never have with her. At that moment, he wanted to be some other guy, the kind who still believed in real love forever.

She tipped her chin up and those leaf-green eyes glittered at him. "Oh, Wes. I feel like I'm bursting out of my skin, I'm so happy. I can't believe it's really happening. I can't thank you enough for everything you've done."

"All I did was get in touch with Glen."

She laid her soft palm against his cheek. "No. You did more. So much more. You listened to me—you really *heard* me—when I told you about Cimarron Rose. And when you went to see Glen, you were able to explain to him exactly what I was looking for."

He chuckled. "It was blind luck that a storefront at the location you want had just become vacant."

"We make our luck, Wes. *You* made luck for me by listening to me, by wanting to help, by going to see Glen." She gave a low laugh. "And it didn't hurt one bit that you're an Abernathy. When you walked into Glen's office, we both know he sat up and took notice. No way I would've gotten the same response."

He held her gaze. "You can't be sure of that."

"Oh, yes, I can."

His mouth twisted wryly. "Well, if my name got you what you need, so be it. But I will make a prediction, Everlee Roberts. The day will come when the Glen Dobsons of this world will be lining up to do business with you."

She laughed again. "Now you sound like my dad."

"He's a very smart man, your dad."

She put her hand against his heart and whispered, "Kiss me again, Weston Abernathy." He gathered her close and lowered his mouth to hers.

The next morning, Wes and Archie were out before dawn. After early chores and breakfast, he and the pup joined up with Garrett and Tyler to cut several acres of alfalfa.

Around three, Wes and Archie returned to the cabin, where Maddox John sat sprawled in one of the Adirondack chairs on the front porch. Wes and Maddox were running buddies. They'd known each other all their lives.

The John family didn't quite have the clout of the Abernathys, but they owned a good-sized spread, the Double J. Maddox had two brothers and his only sister was this year's Miss Bronco, Charity John.

As for Maddox and Wes, they both enjoyed a good time. A week rarely went by that they didn't head into town together at least once. They would spend the evening sharing pitchers of beer, shooting pool and maybe playing poker. Not lately, though. Maddox had been out of town since the middle of June.

Maddox rose from the chair as Wes came up the steps. "Wow. You got a dog."

"And a good one, too. He's only six months old, but I can leave him on his own without worrying he'll freak out and start chewing the furniture. Not to mention, he's fully house-trained. He aims to please. Say hi to Archie."

Maddox bent to make Archie's acquaintance. "He looks a little like the famous Maggie."

"He's one of that litter she had last December. Beer?"

"You bet."

They went inside, where Wes washed up at the sink and Maddox took two longnecks from the fridge. They pulled out chairs at the table and spent some time catching up.

Maddox did most of the talking. He filled Wes in on his travels and complained about his older brother, Jameson, who was engaged to science teacher Vanessa Cruise, and who would inherit a larger share in the Double J simply because he'd been born first. It was an old complaint for Maddox. It pissed him off that an accident of birth order should make Jameson the favored son.

"Let's head into town," Maddox said after downing the last of his beer. "We'll get a nice steak at

DJ's Deluxe. Then we can go to Doug's, maybe play some pool, meet some good-looking women."

Wes had been planning to stop by the house on Union Street. He'd hoped he might share dinner with Evy, her dad and Lola. He'd imagined driving Evy to Doug's later, hanging out there for the evening and taking her home at closing time.

But Maddox looked like he wanted some company and Wes hadn't called Evy yet to wrangle an invite to dinner. They had no agreement to see each other today. He would see her at Doug's later anyway.

Most important, it just wouldn't be cool to blow off the good friend he hadn't seen in weeks. It had been too long since he and Maddox had hung out.

"I should grab a shower, then," Wes said.

"Go for it. Then let's get a move on, have ourselves some fun."

It was after nine when Wes and Maddox arrived at Doug's.

Wes spotted Evy at once. She was working the floor, keeping all the customers happy. Man, did she look good. There was just something about her. Every time Wes saw her, she'd somehow gotten even prettier than the time before.

She caught sight of him. They shared a smile

and he felt warmth spread out from the center of his chest.

The night had kind of dragged till now, but suddenly Wes felt energized, bursting with excitement, ready for anything.

"Grab a table," he said to his buddy. "I'll ask Evy to bring us some beers."

"Aw, come on. She gets paid to come to us."

Wes waved him away. "I'll be there in a minute." He headed for the bar, where Doug was filling Evy's drink tray with a good-sized order.

She spotted him in the mirror behind the bar and turned to him. "Wes."

He drank her in. She really got to him with those shining eyes and that mouth he couldn't wait to kiss again. "Hi. How've you been?"

"Since last night, you mean?" She laughed, the sound lighting him up inside, making him think of the two of them rocking slow and easy in that swing under the oak tree, holding each other, kissing and whispering together, like they were the only two people in the world. "I've been fine, Wes. Wonderful, as a matter of fact." Her eyes shifted over his shoulder. "Maddox John is giving you the high sign. Looks like he's claimed a pool table."

He glanced back at Maddox, who signaled him over. "Right. Well. Just wanted to say hi."

"I'll be there in a minute to take your order."

"Terrific. See you then." Feeling about twelve years old with his first major crush, he went to join Maddox at the pool table.

Wes was about to make a shot when Evy came to get their order. He heard Maddox ask her for a couple of Coronas. Wes sank his ball—and she was already gone.

They played. Maddox lost. The coins were lined up on the table, so Wes played the challenger. Somewhere in there, Evy delivered their beers and moved on to the next table.

When Wes finally lost, he joined his buddy in a booth along the wall near the door. Maddox had ordered another round. They clinked bottles and drank.

And Maddox leaned close across the table between them. "Why do I get the feeling you've finally got something going with Evy Roberts?"

What could he say? "We've been spending some time together. I took her to dinner and I've been getting to know her little girl and her dad. They're good people. Evy's got career plans. She wants to open a store. I helped her find a good storefront."

Maddox sat back. "I know you always had a thing for her. You never could keep your eyes off her—and I get it. She's hot. But this is…" Maddox let the sentence die a silent death.

"This is *what*?"

"Man, you sound serious about her."

"Look. I like her. I do. What's wrong with that?"

"Well, it's just… Evy Roberts has a kid. You don't want to go there."

Wes groaned and shook his head. "You sound like Garrett."

Maddox knocked back a gulp of beer. He set the bottle down carefully. "How so?"

"Garrett got after me for wanting to get to know Evy. His only real reason was that Evy's got a child. He was all up in my face over it—just like you, right now. I have to say, I don't like it when people get up in my face."

"Whoa, man." Maddox put up both hands, palms out, like Wes had a gun on him. "You are prickly about this."

"Yes, I am. Are you really trying to tell me that any single woman who happens to have kids is off-limits, somehow?"

"Come on, Wes. Don't act like you have no clue what I'm talking about. You can't just have a good time with her and then walk away. Women like her, they have to think about the kid and that means they get expectations that things will get serious. For years you've been telling me you don't *do* serious, that you live *free as the wind*—your words, if I remember right."

This conversation was going nowhere good and

Wes wanted to be anywhere but here. "Look, Maddox. What can I tell you?"

"How about the truth?"

Wes blew out a long, slow breath. "All right. The truth is, I'm pretty gone on her."

The jukebox played and people laughed and shouted greetings at each other. At the pool table, someone racked and took a shot. Balls collided. But Wes and Maddox just sat there, staring at each other—until Maddox leaned across the table to say quietly, even gently, "Listen. All I'm asking is, just give it a little more thought, why don't you? You really shouldn't go there with her if you're not in it for real."

Was he in it for real?

Could he be?

The answer was short and simple: no.

If things got too serious, he would only end up hurting her.

Maddox didn't stop there. "Come on. You're not going to get too attached to anyone, not after Belinda. We both know that. What are you doing here, man? What's going on with you?"

Wes had no answer because Maddox had his number. Really, what *was* he doing here, chasing a beautiful woman he was never going to let himself catch?

He needed to stop this. Cut it clean. Now.

Maddox said, "Why don't we get out of here? Let's try that bar in Bronco Heights for a change."

Wes grabbed his hat off the seat. "You're right. Let's go."

Evy watched as Wes and Maddox walked out. Other than when he first came in, Wes hadn't said a word to her.

And so what? she asked herself angrily as she served fries and nachos to a table of six.

He was out with a friend. He'd said hi to her. It wasn't as though he'd ignored her or anything. Just because he'd dropped in at Doug's didn't necessarily mean he'd come to see her. Pasting on her brightest smile, Evy moved on to take drink orders from the guys at the pool tables.

Much later, at home, after she'd looked in on her peacefully sleeping daughter and finally climbed into her own bed, she tried really hard not to feel sad and let down. Trying didn't do much good, though.

Between those few moments at the bar when he'd seemed so happy to see her and an hour or so later when he left without even saying good-night to her, something had happened with him. Something had changed. She was sure of it. She felt convinced he would be steering clear of her from here on out.

The next day, he made no effort to contact her—

and she didn't reach out to him, either. She missed him way too much. Which was a little silly. It was only Wednesday. Two days before, he'd found her the storefront and they'd spent the evening in the swing out back, kissing and staring up at the stars.

Maybe his staying away was for the best. She didn't need a man in her life complicating everything. Maybe all she had to do right now was nothing, just let it be over with him before it even really got started.

Then, five minutes after she thought how she had to prioritize protecting her poor heart, she would realize that she couldn't just walk away without asking him what had suddenly gone wrong.

If he wouldn't come to her, she would have to seek him out.

But really, she had so much to do now, anyway. At her request, Doug had cut her shifts to four nights a week. She would have Tuesdays off in addition to her usual Sunday and Monday. But even with an extra night off, she had way more to do than there were hours in the day.

Her dad had recommended a contractor he knew to remodel the storefront for her. Lester Butz agreed that he and his crew could start right away.

Evy would need to be at Cimarron Rose in the mornings, to check in with Lester, make sure the work was getting done right. Ordering stock was a nightmare. She should have started building inventory six months ago to be ready for a September opening.

And the licensing, registrations, certifications and permits? They were a whole big project in themselves. The work never ended.

The more she thought about it, the more she started thinking that if Wes had decided to pull away, well, maybe that was for the best.

She didn't sleep well after he walked out Tuesday night, but she got up at nine Wednesday morning anyway. She took Lola to daycare, went to her storefront and consulted with Lester. After her meeting with the contractor, she sat down to map out a game plan for getting her business in shape. That night at Doug's, business was steady. She had no time to obsess over what Weston might be up to.

Thursday, she kept the same schedule. At the store, the constant hammering and the ear-splitting scream of the power saw made her want to scream. Sawdust was everywhere.

By lunchtime she desperately needed a break. She stepped out for a bite to eat—and there was Sadie's Holiday House right next door, all lit up like Christmas in the middle of July.

She couldn't help smiling at the sight of it, thinking of her mom way back in the day. Every year on Black Friday, her mom used to bring her to Holiday

House. They would choose one special ornament in honor of that year and then find themselves unable to resist a bunch of other holiday goodies they couldn't do without. The sweet older lady behind the counter always offered Evy a candy cane no matter what time of year they stopped by.

Her smile a little wider and her spirit somewhat lighter, Evy entered the year-round Christmas store, where everything sparkled, Christmas music played and the air smelled of gingerbread, cinnamon and pine.

"Hi! Welcome!" called a pretty, curvy blonde from behind the counter. "I'm Sadie Chamberlin."

Evy introduced herself. Sadie explained that she'd inherited the store from the original owner, the older lady Evy remembered from all those years ago.

"And you've leased the space next door, right?" Sadie asked.

"That's me. It's my dream location." She described her plans for Cimarron Rose.

"I'll be your best customer," said Sadie. "You wait and see."

Evy chose a few Christmas ornaments. She bought some holiday figurines and she and Sadie exchanged phone numbers. They agreed to meet for coffee one day soon.

Evy felt better about everything after her visit

to the shop next door. It still hurt to think of Wes, but hey. Life goes on.

Friday, she called Lester and told him she wouldn't be arriving at the shop until that afternoon.

She and Lola went to the library together for story time, as usual. Lola seemed upbeat and happy. She'd asked after Wes more than once in the past few hectic days. Evy had made excuses, that Weston was busy and so was she, that they couldn't see him every day. Lola had seemed accepting enough of Evy's explanations, which eased Evy's mind a little.

At the library, Evy lucked out because Shari never got a spare moment to sit down and chat, which meant she had no chance to ask Evy how things were going between her and her new special guy. They did get to steal a minute to say hi. Evy shared the news that she'd leased a storefront in Bronco Valley right next to Sadie's Holiday House. "I'm hoping to have my grand opening in September."

Right there in the middle of the children's section, Shari grabbed her in a hug. "Congratulations!"

"Thanks. I'm really excited."

Right then, two boys came looking for Shari. They wanted more books like *The Diary of a Wimpy Kid*. Shari led them off into the stacks and Evy breathed a sigh of relief that she didn't have to talk about Wes.

That night before work, Evy realized she'd had enough. Yeah, she needed to forget about him. But she *couldn't* forget about him—not without first finding out what went wrong.

She sent him a text, an innocuous one.

Hi! We haven't talked in a few days. Been thinking of you. All is well here. I'm working nonstop to get things going with my store—thank you again for finding it for me. How are you? How's Archie?

As soon as she hit Send, she second-guessed herself. Was the tone all wrong? Did she even want to know what had happened to make him suddenly vanish from her life after pursuing her relentlessly?

Scrunching her eyes shut tight, she swallowed down a groan.

Yes. She did want to know. She wanted to know really, really bad and she probably should have just asked him in that text.

But at least she'd done *something.* And now she needed *not* to obsess over him. She stuck her phone in her purse and didn't let herself touch it again until she left Doug's at two thirty the next morning.

Her silly hand was shaking as she checked her messages—and there it was! A text from Wes!

She actually had to slap her hand over her own mouth to keep from letting out a whoop of sheer joy.

But then she read what he'd sent her.

I'm fine. Archie's doing well. You take care now, Everlee.

Everlee? He was calling her *Everlee* now? Sending her a stilted, dreary, completely unengaging text that could have been written by a complete stranger—or maybe a robot?

Over. It was definitely. *O-v-e-r.* Weston Abernathy was done with her.

And it hurt. A lot.

She hardly slept that night. Saturday, she woke up angry and sad, but she tried her best to put a bright face on things. After breakfast, she and Lola baked brownies.

Later, Evy spent some time ordering from her favorite US wholesalers. They had stock from last fall and winter available that they could ship right away. By carefully combing through the offerings, she found a number of great pieces that beautifully fit the brand she envisioned for Cimarron Rose and didn't look like last year's styles at all.

That night at Doug's, she couldn't stop herself from looking over her shoulder every time a customer came in the door. It was a pitiful, knee-jerk reaction—and completely pointless.

Wes never appeared. By closing time, she had no doubt that she and Wes were *d-o-n-e*.

Evy walked home in the cool, quiet middle of the night trying not to cry, telling herself that at least she hadn't slept with him. She would be over him in no time. And anyway, her life was packed. She could use an extra twenty-four hours in every day. The last thing she needed was some flaky guy to obsess over.

She went home and went straight to sleep. No tossing. No turning, just restful, satisfying sleep.

And when she woke up that morning, feeling completely refreshed, she had come to a decision.

That ridiculous, stiff text of his? It wasn't enough. She needed to find out why he'd pursued her so insistently—and then suddenly turned around and walked away.

Leaving Lola happily sharing breakfast with Owen and Dotty, Evy jumped in her Outback and headed for the Flying A.

It was no surprise that she got there in record time. She'd made a joke of the speed limit the entire way. When she reached Wes's cabin, she slammed on the brakes and snapped to a bone-jangling stop, kicking up a satisfying cloud of dry dirt in the process. Shoving her door wide, coughing as she sucked in a lungful of dust, she jumped out and marched right up to his door.

She knocked loudly. And repeatedly.

No answer.

Next, like some sad stalker, she circled the log structure, peering in each of the first-floor windows as she went. Any second now, she expected one of his brothers or maybe some trusty ranch hand to challenge her, to demand that she leave the Flying A immediately or else.

But nobody appeared. She ended up back on the porch again, where she sank to the top step, braced her elbows on her knees and rested her chin in her hands.

Had she lost her mind? Apparently.

Somehow, she'd gone and let herself get completely seduced by Wes Abernathy. She was wild for the man. She'd never felt this way in her life before.

And now it had all blown up in her face. Somehow, she'd managed to get herself into something so beautiful, and now it was over before it even had a chance to begin.

She let her hands drop between her knees and hung her head. What to do now? She didn't want to leave.

But if he didn't want to see her, well, what in the world was she doing here? She needed to drag herself to her feet and go home where she belonged.

Right then, she heard it—the sound that brought flutters to her belly and hope to her heart, the sound of tires crunching gravel, the rumble of an engine suddenly revving to a roar. Someone had just hit the gas.

Evy snapped her spine straight and opened her eyes just in time to see Wes's muddy crew cab come barreling toward her at breakneck speed.

Chapter Eight

When Wes spotted Evy's little SUV parked in front of the cabin, he managed to keep from flooring it—at first. He tried to remind himself that he needed to be strong and calm and send her on her way.

But his damn heart started beating like it would punch clean through his chest and his hands gripped the steering wheel so hard he thought they'd rip through the leather cover and bend the steel beneath. For days now, since he'd walked out of Doug's behind Maddox, he'd been miserable, barking at anyone who looked at him sideways, feeling like he might just bust out of his own skin.

He missed her. He missed Lola, too. He even missed Owen's ugly mug and Dotty's friendly smile. He'd left Doug's Tuesday night and a giant hole had opened beneath his feet. He'd tumbled down into that hole. Since then, he'd been growling at his brothers, ordering his mom to leave him the hell alone, spending sleepless nights wondering how Evy was doing and missing Lola's nonstop chatter.

Okay, yeah, Everlee Roberts deserved a lifetime of love, beginning with a big ring and a walk down the aisle. And he would never offer anyone that again—not even Evy. But she'd said she had no interest in all that, anyway.

And until she started longing for something he couldn't offer, well…

The words in his head trailed off. Well, *what*, exactly? He wasn't sure. He didn't know. He only knew that she was sitting right there on his front porch, waiting for him. And there was no way in hell he could walk away from that.

He floored it. His pickup took off at warp speed.

Somehow, he managed to slam the brakes hard enough that he skidded to a stop before ramming right into the back of her car. In a split second, he was out of his truck, Archie right behind him.

Slowly, she came to her feet.

"Evy…"

"Wes."

That was the extent of their conversation. By then, he stood right in front of her and words had no meaning. He reached for her, wrapped his arms around her. She snuggled right into him with a plaintive little sigh.

How did she do it? What power did she have? Why did holding her feel like everything that mattered in the world—and more. So much more.

Scooping her high against his chest, he headed for the door. It took a little juggling but he managed to keep hold of her while grabbing the latch and shoving the door wide. Stepping inside, with Archie close on his heels, Wes hooked the door with his boot and swung it shut.

Archie eased past him and kept going into the kitchen, no doubt headed for his water bowl.

As for Wes, he just stood there in front of the door, staring down at the woman he held in his arms, getting lost in those green eyes again—at last, after four endless days and nights of constantly reminding himself that he would never look deep in those eyes of hers again. "Damn, Evy. I've missed you. I tried to do the right thing, to stay away…"

"You just walked out of Doug's, Wes. You walked out without a word and then you pretty much ghosted me," she whispered. "I shouldn't be here."

Treat Yourself with 2 Free Books!

Romance

Wholesome Romance

GET UP TO 4 FREE BOOKS & 2 FREE GIFTS WORTH OVER $20

See Inside For Details

Claim Them While You Can

Claim up to FOUR NEW BOOKS & TWO MYSTERY GIFTS – absolutely FREE!

Dear Reader,

We both know life can be difficult at times. That's why it's important to treat yourself so you can relax and recharge once in a while.

And I'd like to help you do this by sending you this amazing offer of up to FOUR brand new full length FREE BOOKS that WE pay for.

This is everything I have ready to send to you right now:

Try **Harlequin® Special Edition** books featuring comfort and strength in the support of loved ones and enjoying the journey no matter what life throws your way.

Try **Harlequin® Heartwarming™ Larger-Print** books featuring uplifting stories where the bonds of friendship, family and community unite.

Or **TRY BOTH!**

All we ask in return is that you answer 4 simple questions on the attached Treat Yourself survey. You'll get **Two Free Books** and **Two Mystery Gifts** from each series you try, *altogether worth over $20*! Who could pass up a deal like that?

Sincerely,

Pam Powers

Harlequin Reader Service

Treat Yourself to Free Books and Free Gifts.

Answer 4 fun questions and get rewarded.

We love to connect with our readers! Please tell us a little about you...

	YES	NO
1. I LOVE reading a good book.	◯	◯
2. I indulge and "treat" myself often.	◯	◯
3. I love getting FREE things.	◯	◯
4. Reading is one of my favorite activities.	◯	◯

TREAT YOURSELF • Pick your 2 Free Books...

Yes! Please send me my Free Books from each series I select and Free Mystery Gifts. I understand that I am under no obligation to buy anything, as explained on the back of this card.

Which do you prefer?

❑ **Harlequin® Special Edition** 235/335 HDL GRCC
❑ **Harlequin® Heartwarming™ Larger-Print** 161/361 HDL GRCC
❑ **Try Both** 235/335 & 161/361 HDL GRCN

FIRST NAME

LAST NAME

ADDRESS

APT.#

CITY

STATE/PROV.

ZIP/POSTAL CODE

EMAIL ❑ Please check this box if you would like to receive newsletters and promotional emails from Harlequin Enterprises ULC and its affiliates. You can unsubscribe anytime.

SE/HW-820-TY22

"But you are. And I'm so damn glad that you are."

"I'm really angry at you."

"I know. And you have every right to be."

"Yes, I do." Her eyes flashed with defiance. "What is going on with you?"

"I'm single, Evy. That's not going to change."

"What? Did I ask you to marry me?"

"You deserve more. You deserve—"

"Shh." She pressed two fingers to his lips. "Listen. You're right. I deserve a lot of things. Good things. The best things. But right now, this minute? I don't even care. I came here to confront you, to find out what's really up with you. But I just…"

"What, Evy? Say it."

With those long, smooth fingers, she caressed the side of his face. He turned his mouth into her palm and pressed a kiss there. He started to speak again, but she touched her fingertips to his lips and softly commanded him, "Take me to your bedroom, please."

"Evy…"

"Shh. Don't argue."

"Wouldn't think of it. But first…" He swooped in for a kiss. She didn't play shy, just lifted her beautiful mouth and met him halfway.

That kiss…

It was everything—sweet and open, hungry and

deep. Her tongue met his and her hands twined around his neck, her fingers whispering up into the hair at his nape.

He lifted away enough to ask, "What next?"

With a soft laugh, she took the brim of his hat and sent it sailing. It landed on one of the leather armchairs beneath the front window. "The bedroom," she reminded him with a radiant smile.

"Yes, ma'am." He carried her in there and set her feet down on the knotted rug by the bed.

She put her hands on his shoulders and gazed up at him, her expression unsure now. "Wes, I…" Her soft voice trailed off. Had she changed her mind? He wanted to groan in frustration at the thought.

But his mama had raised him better than that. "Listen, now. If you're not feeling right about this, we will just march right back out to the front room and—"

"Wes. No. I'm not changing my mind."

Hallelujah! "You're sure?"

"Yes. I'm a little nervous, but I *want* to."

And he couldn't hold back. Gathering her close, he swooped down and claimed her lips again. Her soft breasts pressed against his chest and her tongue sparred with his. He was so hard he felt like he might just poke a hole through his fly. She smelled of flowers and vanilla, sweet as a rose, tasty as sugar cookies.

As for him, he'd just come in from hauling mineral barrels, riding rough dirt roads from pasture to pasture, trading full ones for empties. He probably smelled like it, too. "I should grab a shower."

She chuckled then. "Are you trying to convince me that you're nervous, too?"

"Mostly, I'm just sweaty."

She leaned close, stuck her nose up under his chin and breathed deep. "You smell like dust and man. That works for me."

"You sure?"

"Positive." She blinked up at him. Twice. And then she caught the corner of her lip between her even white teeth. "I've been on the pill since Lola was born, though truthfully, there's never been any reason for me to be. I'm just, well, very careful. I got pregnant by accident once. Now I want to know I'm protected if I just happen to meet up with irresistible temptation and I find myself wanting to surrender."

"I hear you. I do."

"Good." She combed her fingers through the short hair at his temple. "I would prefer to be *doubly* safe. Is that paranoid?"

"Not at all. It's smart." He pulled his wallet from his back pocket, took out a condom and set it on the nightstand.

"Perfect," she said as he dropped the wallet on the nightstand, too.

But when he looked at her again, her sleek eyebrows had drawn together in a hint of a frown. "What's the matter?"

She gave him a nervous smile. "One minute, I feel ready for anything—and then, a second later, I know I'm completely out of my depth. Wes, I've only been with Lola's dad and it's been several years since then."

Was there ever a woman as beautiful as this one, both inside and out?

Doubtful.

"Evy."

"Hmm?"

"If you're not ready, all you have to do is say so."

"No. I'm ready. I am."

He wished he knew how to ease her mind. "You've got nothing to be nervous about."

She grinned just a little. "And you know this, how?"

"I want you so bad it hurts. All you need to do is keep on looking at me like you are now, keep kissing me like you did a minute ago. Look in my eyes, Evy. Let me make it right for you. Let me make it good."

Her cheeks bloomed with sweet color. "You sound so sure."

"Of course I am. All I want to do is be with you, show you how beautiful you are." He skated a finger down her nose. They stared at each other. How was it that just looking at this woman could be so satisfying?

As he watched, those plump lips of hers turned up in a wicked smile. "So then, what are we doing, standing here fully dressed?"

He let out a low laugh. "Good question."

She held his gaze as she unbuttoned her jeans and took her zipper down.

That did it. As she whipped off her shirt, he started tearing off his clothes. They undressed as fast as they could, both of them tossing shirts, jeans and underwear toward the bedside chair, and then jumping around on one foot to pull off their boots.

Finally, he turned and yanked back the quilt. When he faced her again, she was a vision, standing there in the light of the late-morning sun slanting in through the window, every inch of her body revealed.

He took her hand and pulled her down to the bed, gathering her close so they were skin to skin. She felt so good in his arms, impossibly arousing, unbelievably sweet.

She lifted her mouth and he took it. Time flew away. They kissed, rolling so they were on their sides, kissed again—and then again. She ended up on top, her slim legs folded on either side of him, kissing him as though she would never stop.

He twined his tongue with hers, groaning into her soft, wet mouth, rolling them once more. Taking the top position now, he lifted up enough to gaze down at her. She looked so open, so eager, her mouth slightly parted, her cheeks the deepest, prettiest pink, her hair a dark cloud spread out on the white pillow.

Her full breasts, tipped with dusky pink nipples, tempted him. He took one in his mouth. She moaned encouragements, cradling his head, holding him close to her.

His hand strayed downward. She opened for him, lifting herself, offering him everything. He touched her, stroking her, his mind on fire with the feel of her, the glory of her, right here, naked in his bed with him.

She tossed her dark head on the pillow, sighing his name. Her scent drove him wild, like crushed roses and burnt sugar. He kissed his way down the center of her belly. She had faint stretch marks, silvery white, below her navel. He kissed them, too.

And then he moved lower, wanting nothing so much as to eat her right up. Settling himself between her sleek thighs, he guided her knees wide and kissed the musky center of her, tasting her deeply. Using his fingers, too, he drove her higher.

She clutched his head between her hands and cried out as she came. He rode the high with her, stroking her, kissing her, urging her to reach for the peak. When she hit the crest and went over, he stayed right there with her as she drifted slowly back down to earth.

"Mmm…" She made that sweet little humming sound so softly as he kissed his way up along the center of her body again and reached for the condom. Blinking, she gazed at him through dazed eyes, sex-drunk. He smiled at her. Slowly, with a sigh, she grinned back.

She was more beautiful than ever like this, so open, unguarded. Somehow, he'd expected her to be…what?

More restrained, maybe. Less willing to let go.

"Do you have any idea how gorgeous you are?" he asked as he took the condom from its wrapper.

She laughed, a lazy, sensual sound. "Well, you do keep saying so many lovely things to me, telling me I'm beautiful, I'm perfect, there's no one like me."

"You are. There's not."

"And somewhere along the way, I started to believe you."

"Good. Because I'm telling you the truth." Up on his knees now, he rolled the condom carefully down over his aching length. When he glanced up, she was watching him. "Yep." He gave a slow nod. "You are gorgeous. Absolutely gorgeous."

"Wes. Come here." She reached for him. "Come here to me right now."

He went down to her. Easing those sleek thighs apart, settling between them, he went slow. Nothing had ever felt so good as burying himself inch by inch in her softness. She wrapped her legs around him, hooking her ankles at the small of his back.

They moved together, holding on tight, rolling across the white sheet, sharing long, deep, ecstatic kisses, the kind that never seemed to end. When his finish rolled through him, she cried out, too.

The pleasure pulsed between them, electric, a current of heat and joy that gradually resolved into sweet, perfect satisfaction.

A few minutes later, he withdrew to take care of the condom. When he joined her on the bed again, she held up the sheet for him. They rested on their separate pillows. He caught her hand and she wove her fingers with his. For a while, they just lay there, side by side, staring at the beadboard ceiling.

"It's peaceful here," she said.

He met her eyes. "You like it here, on the Flying A?"

"Yes. Very much."

Already, he wanted to pull her close again, kiss

her everywhere, run his tongue over the places he'd missed the first time. He could stay right here in this bed all day with her, touching her.

Kissing her.

Holding her close.

But then her stomach growled. She laughed at the sound and rolled her body toward him, snuggling closer to him, tucking her head beneath his chin.

He wrapped her up in his arms and kissed her tangled hair. "Did you get breakfast?"

"No. I had more important things on my mind." She tipped her head back. They shared a quick kiss. "I needed to get here, to you, to find out what went so wrong that you walked out of Doug's the other night without so much as a see-you-around. I couldn't take the silence anymore. I wanted to know why, since then, all I've gotten from you is one crappy, lukewarm little text."

He felt about half an inch tall. "I'm sorry."

"And you should be. You should also feed me. But first, you should talk to me."

He rolled to his back again, recaptured her hand, kissed it and pressed it to his chest right over his heart. "At the time, I was thinking it would be best, for you and for Lola, if I just stayed away."

"What made you think that?"

"I know that you deserve more."

She eased her hand from his. "More than you're willing to give, you mean?"

"Yeah."

"Did I say I wanted more?"

"No, but—"

"Wes." She canted up on an elbow. "Let me decide what I deserve, okay? What we have right now, it's just right for me. When the day comes that it isn't, you'll know. I'll *let* you know—and as for my little girl, well, I don't want her hurt. I really don't. I'm not sure how to protect her from that. She's already so fond of you. If you disappear from her life for good, well… That's going to be hard. But let's not get ahead of ourselves, okay? Can we just take it one day at a time, see how it goes?"

He rolled to his side and faced her. Sliding his fingers under her hair, he cradled the back of her neck. Whatever happened in the end, he would never get enough of looking into those eyes of hers—or of kissing her. "You're sure?"

Evy lifted up on an elbow and leaned closer. Her hair spilled around them, brushing his shoulder, tickling the back of his neck. "What I need you to know is that I'm good with how things are, that I still want to be with you. If I start to feel differently, I'll let you know."

He released the breath he hadn't realized he was

holding. "Fair enough. I'm so glad you're here, Evy." His voice kind of cracked as it said it.

She did that to him, made him feel weak, made him feel as if he just couldn't get enough of her. He had a heart made of mush. He'd proved that with Belinda, made a complete fool of himself over that woman. And now he was set on a path to make a fool of himself a second time.

He should call a halt right now.

But he'd already tried that last Tuesday night when he walked out of Doug's. He'd been miserable every moment since. He just wanted to be with her. The future could take care of itself.

"Evy, whatever this is we've got going on between us, I don't want to stop, either. I just thought it would be better for both of us if I walked away."

"And was it?"

"Hell, no. I missed you so much. It's been bad. Really bad."

"It's been bad for me, too." She brushed his hair back from his forehead, her touch light as a breath—and then her stomach chose that moment to complain again.

He pulled her down for one more kiss. "You need to eat. I'll fix you some breakfast."

As she sipped coffee and ate bacon and eggs in Wes's rustic kitchen, Evy felt pretty good about everything. Maybe the two of them weren't meant to be together forever. But she wasn't ready to say goodbye to him yet and he'd made it more than clear that he didn't want to lose her, either.

He was a good man. And however it worked out in the end, he really had taught her something about relationships, about the secrets in her own heart, the ones she'd been keeping from herself.

It had all gone so sadly with Chad. He was the father of her child and yet she really hadn't loved him in the deep, honest way she should have. And he certainly hadn't loved her, though he'd said he did all the time—at first, anyway. In the end, he'd walked away from her and never looked back. Worst of all, he'd walked away from her little girl, too.

And she had let him go. At first, she'd nagged him to visit his daughter. He always said he was sorry. He claimed he would start spending time with Lola soon.

"Soon" never came.

She'd messed up with Chad, made a bad choice, so she'd let wounded pride take over. She'd decided to forget men until later, until she'd raised her daughter, made her shop a reality. She'd told herself she would do fine on her own.

Still, in her deepest heart, she'd never completely given up on love. Someday, she wanted what her parents had shared. The real thing, deep and true, destined to last. She wanted love with the right man.

For now, though?

It was enough. More than enough—to be sitting here in Wes's kitchen, sipping coffee and polishing off her second slice of crispy bacon, stealing glances at the man across the table while Archie rolled around on the floor growling, shaking his favorite chew toy between his teeth.

Wes said, "We should go get Lola." That made her smile. He really did like Lola. Not only was the guy amazing in bed, but he also treated her daughter right. Chad could learn a thing or two from Wes about how a good man behaved. "Evy?"

She was lost in thought. "Hmm?"

"Let's go get Lola. What do you say?"

"Works for me."

They took Archie in the crew cab and drove into town. Lola ran out to greet them when they pulled up in front of the house. Wes asked her if she'd like to spend the day at the ranch. She was so excited to get going, she changed into jeans, sturdy boots and a T-shirt in three minutes flat.

"It's a warm day," Wes said before they left. "We just might go for a swim in Little Big Bear Creek."

Evy packed their suits and beach towels and off they went.

Back at the Flying A, Lola got to ride slowly

around the horse pasture on Babycakes. Wes took them swimming a few miles from the cabin at a nice, wide spot in the creek. Later, they all three ended up just relaxing on the front porch. Evy shared stories of her progress pulling her store together while Lola played with Archie, looked at her books and fiddled on her pink kid's tablet. By four, she was yawning.

"I just need a little rest," she declared. Evy took her inside and she stretched out on the sofa, put her head on a throw pillow and closed her eyes. Her breathing evened into sleep almost instantly.

Evy tucked an afghan around her and went back outside to rejoin Wes on the front porch. It was nice, just being together out of the heat of the late afternoon.

His mother, Hannah, came by in a pickup. She greeted Evy warmly and invited them—Lola, too— up to the main house for dinner.

"What do you think?" Wes asked. He seemed pleased at the idea.

But why wouldn't he be? He'd already made himself right at home at Evy's house. It really didn't have to mean anything these days, when a guy brought a girl home to dinner with the parents. Still, dinner at the main house felt like a big step to Evy.

She thanked Hannah, but said she needed to get

back to town soon. It was true enough, as far as it went. Evy wanted to be in bed early tonight so she could get to work at her store first thing in the morning.

Beyond her goals with the store, she needed to keep things in perspective with Wes. Yes, she'd come after him when he'd walked away from her. She'd climbed into bed with him. Maybe she shouldn't have done that, but she had and she owned it. She refused to regret it. They were in it for right now as long as it worked for both of them.

She and Wes stood at the top of the porch steps and waved as Hannah drove away.

Once his mom's pickup had disappeared from sight, Wes turned to Evy. "Stay. Maybe dinner with my family is a little more than you're up for, but we could fix something to eat here at the cabin, just the three of us."

Perspective, she reminded herself. *Just keep yourself from getting in too deep.* "No, really. I need to get going."

"But you've got tomorrow off, too."

"True—and Doug also gave me Tuesday nights off. From now on, I work four nights a week. Which is wonderful. I'm not kidding, there aren't enough hours in a day. Everything needs doing yesterday."

He stepped closer and took her by the arms. "How about dinner out, you and me, tomorrow night? Someplace nice. The Association. Or maybe Coeur de l'Ouest. It's cozier and the food is amazing."

Coeur de l'Ouest was not what Evy would call cozy. Intimate, definitely. And exclusive and very expensive. Everyone said the food was out of this world.

And she couldn't help thinking that for a guy who didn't want to get too close, he sure seemed eager to spend every moment he could with her. "So you missed me when you dumped me, huh?" The words were out before she realized she would say them.

He had the grace to look guilty. "You're still mad at me."

"No, I'm not. But I'm not going to lie. It hurts that you walked away without a word. I got crickets from you except for that text."

He winced. "Didn't we already talk about this?"

"Yes, we did. And I want to be over it, but I guess I'm just not."

He studied her face as though he needed to memorize it. "I'm so gone on you, Evy. It freaked me out."

"So, then, you like me so much, you cut me loose and you didn't even tell me what was up with you before you did it. Communication goes a long way, Wes."

"You're right. I get that. It was a dick move to

walk out. And then I missed you so much, I thought I would go nuts. All I could think about was you. And then this morning, here you were. Evy, the sight of you sitting right here on the top step, waiting for me... Talk about a great moment. Now I'm kind of afraid to let you out of my sight."

She could not resist razzing him a little. "You know, you sound like a guy who's getting way too serious."

He took her by the shoulders. "Please. Go out with me tomorrow night."

"Sorry. Tomorrow night, I'm going to knock off at the store early and get a little girl time with Lola."

"Tuesday night, then?"

She almost laughed. "Why do I feel like I'm not getting through to you?"

He pulled her right up against him and stole a slow kiss. When he lifted his head, he asked, "So that's a yes for Tuesday night?"

She did laugh then. "I think you finally wore me down. But I don't want to go out. Come have dinner at my house Tuesday night. Six o'clock. If you're lucky there might even be Tater Tots in it for you."

Evy's dad couldn't look after Lola the next day. He had a man out sick at The Plumbing Professionals. Dotty was unavailable, too. She'd gone to Billings to visit her daughter and grandbabies. Evy took Lola to daycare and then headed for her store, where the day flew by much too fast.

At three thirty, the internet and phone guy had yet to appear. Rescheduling wasn't an option— not as far as Evy was concerned. With Wi-Fi, she could do so much right there on-site. She could track down more inventory, get the website spruced up for launch, pull everything together, all while keeping an eye on the progress of the remodel. Plus, she had one more delivery coming today and she would need to sign for it.

She was pacing back and forth in front of the new display shelving, her phone to her ear, waiting to leave yet another urgent voice mail for her dad, when someone tapped on the wide front window.

Wes.

He tipped his hat at her as she dropped her phone on a shelf and went to let him in. Archie, on a leash, sat panting at his feet. "Are dogs allowed?"

She grinned down at the big puppy, who cocked an ear and panted up at her hopefully. "Service dogs only, after we open. But we're not open yet. Plus, it's Archie, so I'll make an exception."

He led the dog in and she shut the door. "I was in town. Thought I'd drop by, see how you're doing."

"Couldn't stay away, huh?" she teased.

He and Archie shared a look and Wes admitted, "Yeah, pretty much."

Gently, she reminded him, "It's just Lola and me tonight, Wes. I'm not changing my mind."

"I know, I know." He gave her his sexiest half grin. "Don't rub it in." He glanced around the space. "Things are looking up around here."

"There's still way too much to do, though—hold on." She grabbed her phone and tried her dad again. Again, it went straight to voice mail.

Wes was watching her. "What's going on?"

"The phone and internet guy *and* a delivery I'm expecting are both running late. I need to be here to deal with all that. But I told Lola I would pick her up at four. She's looking forward to our girls' night and I hate to disappoint her. My dad would go get her, but I can't seem to reach him. According to one of the guys who works for him, he went home at noon. But he's not answering his phone or the landline at home—which worries me a little. He always gets right back to me when I call."

"Maybe Dotty could—"

"I wish. Dotty is out of town."

"Well, then. I'll go get Lola. I'll take her to your house. If Owen's not there, I'll keep her busy until he gets there, or until you come home."

Relief eased the tension between her shoulder blades. "I shouldn't take advantage of you this way."

He was grinning that grin again. "But you're going to do it anyway and hey, it's a win for me. I get to see Lola and it's looking like you might be serving me Tater Tots a night early. Plus, Archie can't wait to get himself some quality time with Valentina. Right, Arch?" Archie barked on cue.

She let herself breathe easier. "I owe you."

"Hmm. Yes, you do. Tonight, in addition to the Tater Tots you promised me, I'll be expecting some time on that porch swing out back."

Ten minutes later, Wes parked in the daycare center's lot. Evy had given him her house key. She'd also called the daycare and arranged it so that Wes could take Lola home.

Lola was waiting for him when the daycare director showed him to her classroom. "Weston!" she chirped and reached for his hand. "My mommy called and said you were picking me up. Come on. You can meet my friends."

She towed him around the room, pointing out a couple of pictures she'd drawn and an art project that consisted of dried macaroni and brightly colored yarn glued onto a paper plate to form a picture of a little girl's face. "This is my very good friend Weston," she announced to a group of kids playing with blocks in one corner. She said it again to two boys about her age who were pretending to roast a plastic chicken in a toy oven.

Once they'd circled the sunny classroom, she

stopped and peered up at him. "Okay. We can go home now." She waved and called out goodbyes as they went out the door.

"Archie!" She exclaimed in glee when Wes helped her up into the back seat of his truck. After hugging and petting the dog, she clambered into the car seat Evy had transferred from her Subaru before Wes left Commercial Street. In a flash, Lola had herself belted in. "Okay, Weston. I'm ready. Let's go!"

During the drive home Lola explained to him that she still hoped to get her nails painted even though her mom would be late getting home. "If Pop-Pop's not there, you'll have to do it, Weston. But that's okay. I'll paint yours for you. Weston?"

He met her green eyes in the rearview mirror— man, those eyes. Just like her mama's. "Hmm?"

"I hope you like playing dress-up, too."

She was too cute and he'd probably end up doing whatever she told him to do. "Can't wait."

They turned the corner onto her street and he spotted the blue van with The Plumbing Professionals logo on the side. "Looks like your pop-pop is home."

"But you will stay anyway and we can play dress-up. Right, Weston?"

Worked for him. The sudden appearance of Owen Roberts would not be messing up his plan to get Tater Tots for dinner and some quality time with Evy in the swing out in back. "You bet I will."

Lola was already out of her seat when he opened the door for her. He hooked Archie's leash back on his collar. She grabbed her *Mulan* backpack in one hand and his index finger in the other. Up the front walk they went.

He had the key Evy had given him, but if Owen happened to be there now, he didn't want to startle the poor guy by barging right in. Gently, he pulled his finger from Lola's grip and rang the doorbell.

After a minute, Lola tapped the toe of her pink cowboy boot. "Pop-Pop is taking a *really* long time."

Wes rang again.

Nothing.

Lola gazed up at him, button nose wrinkled in a puzzled little frown. "Maybe he's sleeping, Weston."

"Could be." He pulled Evy's key from his pocket, opened the door—and hesitated before going in.

Not Lola. She bounced across the threshold as her kitten peeked around the wall from the family room. "Tina!" The cat came right to her. She dropped her pack and scooped up the furry little thing. Wes led Archie inside. He was shutting the door as Lola called, "Pop-Pop, I'm home and Weston's here, too!"

No answer at first—but then, faintly from down the long hall that branched to the bedrooms, Wes heard a groan followed by Owen's strained voice. "Lollipop, honey, you stay right there and send Weston down here, please."

Lola whirled back to face him. Eyes wide as hubcaps, she whispered, "Pop-Pop doesn't sound very good."

Wes clasped her small shoulder. "Let me go see what I can do. You take Archie and Valentina into the family room and keep an eye on them, okay?"

"But what about Pop-Pop?" She was still whispering.

"I'll just check on him and be right back."

"You promise?"

"I do." He handed her Archie's leash and she took the animals into the other room.

Wes glanced into each empty room as he walked down the hall. At the end, across from the pink-and-purple room that had to be Lola's, Owen Roberts, his face kind of gray and his hand clutching his belly, lay sprawled on the bed in his work shirt and khakis.

Chapter Nine

Wes tapped on the door frame. "Owen? How're you doing?"

Owen lifted his head and dropped it back to his pillow with another groan. "Not good. It's food poisoning, I think. I knew that hoagie was off." He winced, clutched his belly and tipped his head toward the phone on the nightstand. "House phone's giving me a busy signal and I put my cell phone down somewhere…"

Wes opened his mouth to ask how he could help, but before he got a word out, Owen's eyes popped wide. "Hold on!" He groaned as he rolled off the bed. His feet hit the floor and he was off, racing to the en suite bathroom, slamming the door behind him as soon as he got there.

Wes took out his phone and looked up *Food Poisoning.* As he read about dosing with acidophilus, Pepto-Bismol and lots of liquids, Owen reappeared looking like death warmed over.

"Sorry 'bout that..." He staggered back to the bed and fell across it.

"Weston!" It was Lola.

"Don't let her come down here," Owen commanded and then started groaning again.

Wes stuck his head out the bedroom door. Lola stood at the other end of the hall with Archie at her side. Both the little girl and the dog looked apprehensive.

"Go see if she's okay," growled Owen from the bed. "Shut the door when you go."

"Be right back," he promised, and pulled the door shut.

"Is Pop-Pop okay?" Lola asked.

Wes went to her. "He's not feeling well right now, but he'll be all right by tomorrow or the next day. Don't worry."

"I should go see him."

"In a little while." Wes took her hand. "Let's fix you a snack. While you're eating, we'll call your mommy and then I'll go and see how your pop-pop is doing."

A few minutes later, Lola sat at the table alternately eating apple slices and Goldfish crackers. Archie was stretched out at her feet and her kitten had curled up in a ball on the nearby family room sofa.

Wes found a cell phone on the peninsula counter that marked off the business side of the kitchen. Next to the cell lay the handset of the wall phone. Owen must have left it off the hook. Wes hung it up and called Evy from his own phone.

"Wes?" She sounded a little frantic. "Is everything okay?" Quickly, he brought her up to speed.

"Oh, no. Poor Dad."

"He'll be okay."

"I can't thank you enough." She said it softly.

"Anytime. How are things on your end?"

"Not great. Still no sign of the Wi-Fi guy. And at this point, I don't even care what happens to that delivery. I'm coming home right now."

"Don't give up now. Stay. Your dad will be fine. He just needs rest and lots of liquids. Lola's having a snack. Everything's under control."

"I should be there."

"Honestly. You can't do any more here than I'm doing. I'm on this, Evy, and I'll stick around here as long as I'm needed."

"But it's not right to take advantage of you like this."

"You're not taking advantage. Get your stuff done. I'll be here when you get home."

"You're sure?"

"Positive."

"Weston!" Lola waved a half-eaten apple slice at him. "Please can I talk to my mommy?"

He gave her the phone. She started right in on a wide range of subjects from her daycare adventures to Archie to Pop-Pop feeling sick and Weston "promising" to paint her fingernails and play dress-up with her.

Apparently, Evy finally managed to interrupt the chatter. Lola chirped brightly, "Okay! Bye, Mommy. I love you." Lola held out the phone to Weston.

It was sticky.

So what? He put it to his ear. "Hey."

"Thank you, Wes. So much."

He felt like a superhero. "No problem. I'm getting time on the swing out under the stars and two fancy dinners here at your house. Happy to help."

She thanked him again and they said goodbye.

He stuck his phone in one pocket and Owen's in the other. Then he headed for the fridge, where he found a six-pack of ginger ale. That should help keep the older man hydrated.

Before he went back down the hall, he took Archie off the leash and got Lola's agreement that when she finished her snack, she would go into her room and play with her tablet or her toys. He had no idea how long a lively four-year-old would stick to such an agreement. But he would worry about her attention span when it became an issue. Right now, he had poor Owen to deal with.

Armed with a glass of water in one hand and a ginger ale in the other, he headed down the hall.

Owen looked as pasty-faced and miserable as before. Wes helped him get into pajamas and then under the covers. He put Owen's phone on the bedside table within easy reach and reassured him that the landline was working again, too. While Owen sipped ginger ale, Wes asked some crucial questions he'd found online, the ones designed to determine if the older man should head for the hospital or at least call his doctor.

"It's just plain old food poisoning," Owen insisted.

"I think you're probably right. You have Pepto-Bismol?" Owen had it. Wes dosed him with it.

As Wes plumped the pillows, Owen asked, "What did you do with my daughter?"

Wes explained about the late delivery and the Wi-Fi guy.

"You're all right, son," declared Owen. "Not good enough for my baby girl, but then, no man is."

Wes did not disagree. "Drink your liquids and rest. I'll be back to check on you soon."

He exited the bedroom and saw Lola waiting for him at the end of the hall. "Weston! Is Pop-Pop all better?" She had one hand behind her back.

"He's getting there—and what's that you're hiding?"

"Surprise!" She whipped that hand out in front of her to reveal a bottle of nail polish the exact turquoise color of the '65 Ford Galaxie 500 his great-uncle Chester used to drive. "Come on, Weston. I will paint yours first."

When Evy finally arrived home, she found her dad on the family room sofa looking wrung out as Lola attempted to read to him from one of her library books. Archie had made himself comfortable under the coffee table and Wes stood at the stove with a slotted spatula in one hand. With the other, he stirred something in a pot.

"Mommy!" Lola dropped her book on the coffee table and held up her arms. "Hug!"

Evy scooped her up and held her close. "How are you feeling?" she asked her dad.

"Not great. I'm still primed to bolt down the hall

if I have to, but at least now I'm starting to think I might survive."

Lola pulled back a little, enough to frame Evy's face between her small hands. "Everything is all fine, Mommy. Pop-Pop's feeling a little bit better and Weston is making grilled cheese and tomato soup for us and broth for Pop-Pop because Pop-Pop had some poison in his food."

From over at the stove, Weston asked, "You get your Wi-Fi hooked up?"

She met his eyes, thinking how great he looked standing in her kitchen, stirring soup and flipping sandwiches. Okay, so maybe he had issues with love and all that, but so did she. And he certainly had stepped right up and saved the day when she needed him. Plus, his kisses lit her up like a four-alarm fire. Wes Abernathy was a good man, all the way to the bone.

And right now, she had this lovely, bubbly, lifting feeling. Like happiness. Pure happiness.

He gave her a sideways look and she realized she hadn't answered him about her problems at the store.

"Everything's handled, thank you. Finally."

"That's what I wanted to hear."

"Mommy, you can put me down now."

She let Lola wriggle to the floor and said to Wes, "I'll set the table."

"We're eating at the coffee table," Lola announced. "Weston said we could."

Evy shot another glance at the man by the stove.

He shrugged. "Hey. It seemed like a good idea to keep Owen company."

Her dad scoffed. "Yeah, I'll be really lonely lying here on the sofa while you guys eat dinner at the table ten feet away."

Evy bent, kissed his forehead and smoothed back his thinning hair. "I'll just wash my hands, then, and we'll set the coffee table."

"I'll help!" Lola sang out.

And she did. She put out the placemats and carefully folded the paper napkins into triangles. The three of them sat on the floor while Evy's dad, propped up on pillows against the armrest, sipped slowly from a mug of beef broth. Lola kept slipping Archie bits of her sandwich under the table.

Evy let her do it. Mostly because right at that moment, Wes took a bite of his sandwich and she saw that someone—most likely a certain four-year-old—had given him a manicure. "Tropical Aqua." She grinned. "My favorite color."

He set down his sandwich and wriggled his fingers at her. The polish had gotten on more than just his nails. "Lola hooked me up."

Lola beamed. "We played dress-up for a while and we had to take care of Pop-Pop, so we didn't have time for Weston to do mine, but I said it would be okay because you could do mine when you got home."

After the meal, Evy fully expected Wes to say he had to get going. He'd been dealing with food poisoning and Lola for hours now. Naturally, she assumed the man would need a break.

He stayed. Owen returned to his bedroom for the night. Lola got ready for bed and then Evy painted her nails petal pink. While Lola's polish dried, the three of them sat on the sofa in the front room off the entry hall. They watched an episode of *Backyardigans* on the big-screen TV Evy's dad had bought the year before.

By eight fifteen, Lola was all tucked in bed with her kitten. Evy quietly pulled her little girl's bedroom door almost shut, leaving it open just enough for Tina to get out. Next, she peeked in on her dad, who was still awake, watching one of those home improvement shows, the kind where a burly contractor renovates a whole house for a grateful young couple.

"'Night, Dad. Feel better."

"'Night, sweetheart."

Evy shut his door.

Wes and Archie were waiting in the family room. Evy led them outside, where she and Wes sat on the swing. Archie romped around on the grass for a while, chasing shadows, and ended up lying down near their feet.

Wes cradled Evy in the circle of his arm and she put her head on his shoulder. Today had been one disaster after another, yet somehow, right now, life felt just about perfect. She didn't want the evening to end.

It was almost full dark when she took his hand and pulled him out of the swing. He started to speak, but she brought a finger to her lips and shook her head.

They went inside with Archie following behind them. He really was a great dog, so eager to do the right thing, to make his humans happy. Being left behind by the first family to adopt him hadn't made him troublesome. It had only made him try harder. Evy couldn't help thinking that everyone could take a lesson from that.

In the family room, she commanded, "Stay."

The pup stretched out on the rug by the sofa.

"This way." Evy took Wes's hand and led him down the darkened hallway to her room, letting go only after she'd pulled him inside.

Quietly, she shut the door and engaged the privacy lock. She could feel Wes standing right behind her, the warmth of him, the steady strength. He liked to think of himself as lighthearted, easy-going. And he was. But he was also generous and caring, tender in a deep and real way.

And right now, she longed only for his arms around her.

Turning to face him, she whispered, "Excuse me." He gave her a puzzled frown, but he did step aside. She went to her bed, flipped on the lamp and folded the covers back.

Wes hadn't moved from his spot near the door. "What's going on?"

She whirled to face him. "Shh." She whispered and crooked a finger. "Come here."

"Evy…" He was whispering too, now. "Your dad's across the hall. Your daughter's in the room next door."

As if she didn't know the layout of her own house. "I'm aware."

"Then what are you doing?"

"Isn't it obvious?"

He looked completely bumfuzzled—and also killer handsome in his dark-wash Wranglers and a black T-shirt that showed off his broad chest and strong arms. "You really think this is a good idea?"

She braced her fists on her hips. "Are you staying or going? Make up your mind."

"But your dad…"

"My dad's not going to know. It's not his business. However…"

His dark eyebrows crunched together. "What? Say it."

"We'll have to be quiet. Very, very quiet. You think you can manage that?"

He seemed to relax a little then. One corner of his mouth twitched in a near-smirk. He looked her slowly up and down. "You are the most surprising woman."

I love you, Weston Abernathy.

The words just popped into her head. Somehow, she kept from saying them.

Really, she had to watch herself, keep things in perspective. What they had was so good, but calling it love?

Her heart started racing at the very thought. No way was she ready for love. Not for years yet, if ever. And besides, she hadn't spent enough time with him to know that she loved him.

But she did think the world of him. Since the night that rock came flying through the window at Doug's, the night Wes leapt to her rescue, he'd knocked himself out making sure she had what she wanted, what she needed. He'd found her store for her. Her daughter adored him. And today, he'd insisted on looking after her family while she took care of business at Cimarron Rose.

She knew he had a big heart, a heart that spoke to her heart. And whatever happened later, she wanted to make the most of whatever time they had together.

But love?

Uh-uh. That was too much, too soon. She didn't love him and he'd made it perfectly clear he wasn't in the market for love, either.

"Can you be really quiet, Wes?"

He squared his broad shoulders and closed the distance between them. Now his eyes were twin blue flames. "I can sure as hell try."

"Kiss me, then."

He didn't need to be told twice. His mouth covered hers and she surged up, sliding her hands over his hard chest, linking them behind his neck. That kiss went on and on. She wished she could make it last forever.

Too soon, he lifted his head and looked down at her. "Evy?"

"Hmm?"

"You're sure about this, now?"

"Oh, yes, I am."

"Well, then. Let's get you out of these clothes."

"Great idea." She was unbuttoning her ruffled shirt as she spoke.

He held out a hand for it. She passed it to him, followed by her pretty concho belt and her knitted calf-length boho skirt. He carefully laid each item across her bedside chair.

In no time, she was naked except for her high-heeled tan boots. He guided her to sit on the bed, swept to a crouch and took those boots off. Rolling down her soft socks, he took them, too.

Rising, he pulled a condom from his wallet and set it beside the lamp. Then he started whipping off his own clothes. Tossing everything to the floor, he dropped to the bed beside her to yank off his boots and socks.

She just sat there, buck naked, watching him, loving the wiry, hard strength of him, admiring that sexy V at the base of his lean torso, appreciating the tempting, silky line of dark hair pointing the way down to his straining erection.

He reached for her. Scrambling up to her knees, throwing a leg across his lap, she straddled him, wrapping her arms and legs around him. He kissed her and she opened to him eagerly. For a while, they did nothing but share kisses and whisper to each other, a couple of naughty kids up to no good and enjoying every second of their mutual bad behavior.

Reaching between them, she trailed two fingers down that silky line of hair on his belly. Wrapping her hand around him, she stroked him. Swallowing a groan, he fell back across the bed, taking her down with him.

She didn't stay put, though. Easing off him to

her knees, she bent over him and took him in her mouth.

His groans got louder. Walking her fingers back up that trail of hair along the center of his whip-lean body, she covered his mouth with her hand.

"Okay," he whisper-groaned against her palm. "I'm quiet. So quiet. I promise… Evy. Please. Just don't stop."

And she didn't stop. When he warned her that he was about to lose it, she didn't pull away. She wanted all of him. She wanted to make it good for him. She stuck with him as he came. The taste of him, both salty and sweet, flooded her mouth. She swallowed it down.

A few minutes later, he gathered her close and tucked her in against his side. She rested her head on his shoulder and put her hand against his chest to feel his heart beating so hard and deep, slowing a little as he caught his breath again.

Carefully, he combed his fingers through her tangled hair as he peppered her with kisses on her forehead, her nose, at the corner of her eye. She let herself go loose and boneless in his arms and al-most dropped off to sleep.

But then he cradled her breast in his big palm and her body heated.

It started all over again.

When he reached out to feel for the condom on the nightstand, she whispered, "Let me."

He handed it to her. Rising, she claimed the top position and straddled him. His eyes gleamed up at her. She loved the way he looked at her, as though she was everything, all that mattered in the world.

Her hands only shook a little as she removed the wrapper and rolled the condom down over him. Lifting up, she guided him to where she wanted him. Slowly, she lowered herself, taking him in. She was wet and eager. Her body welcomed him.

With him, making love felt so right.

"Evy, what you do to me..." His eyes were oceans, drowning her.

She rocked on him, holding him deep, setting the rhythm. It was so beautiful with him, exactly the way it should be, between a woman and the man for her.

I love you, Wes. Love you, love you...

The words filled her head. She denied them, shoved them down, banished them. It was too soon and she wasn't ready. And as for him, he'd warned he would never be ready.

She needed to accept that.

She *did* accept that.

And right now, holding him inside her, moving with him in perfect rhythm, she felt truly happy. She was exactly where she needed to be.

She knew she'd made the right decision to go after him yesterday, to be waiting on his front porch when he came roaring toward her in his muddy crew cab. It was good that she'd sought him out—that they'd given give this magic between them another chance.

"Evy…" He groaned her name as he rolled them and took the top position.

She wrapped her legs around his lean hips, hooking her ankles at the small of his back. He surged within her. She clutched him so tightly. They moved together, slow and deep, then fast and hard.

Within moments, her fulfillment found her. It took form deep inside her, throbbing so sweetly, vibrating outward like the ripples in a pond.

She moaned his name. There was nothing but pleasure.

Nothing but Wes, holding her, rousing her, taking her over the edge of the world and then following right after her, pulsing inside her as he found his finish, until both of them lay limp with satisfaction.

"I'll be right back," he promised as he left the bed to dispose of the condom.

When he returned to her, they cuddled under the covers, whispering together, reminding each other that they needed to be quiet, that he should go.

Still, he stayed.

They talked of nothing, really. Just silly things,

inconsequential things. It was so good, so sweet. So exactly right.

She couldn't stop herself from thinking that he was everything she wanted in a man and all her daughter needed in a dad.

Stop, she reminded herself silently. *Don't go there*.

And he said, "I should go," for the tenth time that night.

"I know…" She snuggled in close to him.

She must have drifted off to sleep.

When she woke, morning sun peeked through the blinds and she was alone in her bed. She sat up and stretched. It was a little before ten. She felt deeply content, perfectly rested—and she needed to check on her dad and her daughter.

But first, what about Wes?

She rolled her head toward the nightstand and saw that he'd left her house key beside the lamp. Tossing back the covers, she slipped naked from the bed and peered out the window that faced the front of the house. His truck, parked at the curb when she got home from her shop yesterday, was gone.

She missed him already, but she grinned to herself as she pictured him and Archie sneaking out the front door in the middle of the night. Sinking to the edge of the mattress, she thought about the night before, about the two of them, together right here in her bed. The memory had her sighing in happiness, staring blindly into the middle distance, a silly grin on her face.

The grin turned to a frown as she remembered her poor dad.

Was he better this morning or still suffering? And what about Lola? Most days, Lolly was up by eight at the latest. She always had Owen to look after her until Evy emerged from her room.

Jumping up, she put on sleep shorts and a big T-shirt. She slipped her feet into plush open-toed slippers and stuck her head out into the hallway. Her dad's bedroom door stood open. Lola's did, too. And now she could hear Lola, out in the kitchen or maybe the family room, chattering away.

When she emerged from the hallway, she saw that Wes had even remembered to bring in Lola's car seat. He'd left it on the family-room sofa. She found her dad sitting at the breakfast table, glasses perched on the end of his nose, reading the *Bronco Bulletin* and sipping coffee.

Lola sat one chair away from him on her booster seat, eating packaged cereal. "Mommy! You're up!"

Evy went straight to her and gave her a kiss on her sticky cheek. "Good morning."

"Good morning, Mommy!"

Evy's dad was a step away. "Feeling better?"

She pressed her palm to his forehead. His skin was cool, no fever.

"I'm getting there." He looked haggard, the lines on his forehead deeper than usual, dark circles under his eyes.

"Did you eat?"

He put up a hand. "Not quite ready for solid food yet. I had juice." He saluted her with his coffee mug. "And there's coffee. Help yourself."

She went to the pot and filled a mug. "Tell me you're planning to stay home today." She took the chair across from Lola.

Owen gave her a weary smile. "Yes, Everlee. I'm staying home today."

"That's good, Dad. You need to take it easy."

"Will do."

Lola glanced from her mother to her pop-pop and back to Evy again. "Am I going to daycare?"

"Yes, you are. I'll drop you off on the way to my shop."

"Okay! It's a swim day. I like swimming." Lola's daycare had a pool. All the kids loved swim days.

Evy's dad was watching her. He arched a bushy eyebrow. "How did you sleep, sweetheart?"

"Like a baby." She flashed him a giant smile.

"What time did Weston take off?"

"It was late. We spent hours out on the backyard swing, just talking, you know?"

"Ah," said her father. He had a look that said he knew exactly what the two of them had been up to till all hours of the night. "Say no more. I get it. I was young once, too, you know…"

That evening, the doorbell rang at six o'clock sharp. *Wes*. Evy's heart raced with gladness as Lola ran to answer.

They had burgers, tossed salad—and Tater Tots, too. Dotty, back from Billings, came across the street to eat with them. She fussed over Evy's dad, who seemed mostly recovered. Especially his appetite. Owen ate two burgers and more than his share of Tater Tots.

Wes stayed for a couple of hours after Lola went to bed. He joked that his brothers had been giving him a hard time about his turquoise fingernails. She offered to get the polish remover and solve the problem.

He laughed. "No way. Tropical Aqua is my color."

They sat out on the porch swing, chatting quietly, sharing kisses. He left too soon. She missed him the moment his taillights disappeared around the corner.

But Wednesday night, he showed up late at Doug's. They canoodled in his truck for an hour after closing like a couple of hormone-addled teenagers.

Thursday night, very late, she snuck him into the

house. They made frantic, amazing love—quietly, she hoped. It was hard to be quiet when his every kiss and tender touch set her body on fire.

When he left, she pulled on her sleep shorts and a T-shirt and tiptoed with him to the door.

He grabbed her close for one last kiss. "I don't want to go. I never want to go. I want to be right here with you, touching you, all the time." He kissed her with urgency. They'd just made love twice, but she wanted to drag him back down the hall and do it again.

The dangerous, impossible words were suddenly right there, on the tip of her tongue. *I love you, Wes...*

He chuckled then. For a moment, she was sure she'd actually said it out loud. But then he whispered, "You should see your face. Like you've seen a ghost."

You have no idea. "Shut up." She went on tiptoe and took his mouth in a blazing-hot kiss.

When she dropped back to her heels, he pressed his forehead to hers. "Now I *really* don't want to go."

"Too bad."

"You're a cruel, cruel woman, Evy Roberts."

"Out. I mean it. It's really late."

He dropped a last kiss on her nose and left. She shut and locked the door behind him and then sagged back against it.

Dear Lord, she really needed to get a grip on herself. He didn't want love and she wasn't ready for it. They had a great thing going, for now. She would relish every minute they had together and stop thinking like some romantic fool.

Friday, Dotty took Lola to the library for story time. Evy ran errands and spent a few hours at Cimarron Rose adding content to the website, ordering more stock, consulting with her contractor on the progress of the remodel.

Her new friend Sadie dropped by. Evy gave her a quick tour of the shop, describing what it would look like once the remodel was completed as they went. Sadie suggested lunch. They had iced café mocha lattes and packaged club sandwiches at Bean & Biscotti across the street.

That day, Wes and his brothers had to drive some cattle up to higher pastures. He'd told Evy that they would spend that night under the stars, so she didn't see him at Doug's.

It was only one night without him. She missed him anyway. The hours seemed to drag by in slow motion. She missed the anticipation of the moment he would walk in the door, the whole-body shiver she got when he first moved in close and said her name, all quiet and soft. She longed for that private smile he gave her every time she glanced his way.

Saturday night, he showed up at Doug's just before closing. She glanced toward the door—which she'd done far too many times that evening—and there he was, grinning right at her. She wanted to run to him, throw her arms around him and kiss him until he begged for mercy. Somehow, she controlled herself, though just barely.

After closing, she had him drive her straight home. They spent two hours in her bed making beautiful, wild, mostly silent love.

Sunday, she didn't have to work. She and Lola drove out to the Flying A to share the morning and early afternoon with Wes. Before they left, Wes asked Evy out to dinner at The Association. This time, she said yes to the fancy dinner at the place where all the rich ranchers hung out.

Before Wes came to pick her up, she talked to her dad and explained that she was hoping he might watch Lola overnight.

He hugged her and then took her by the shoulders and held her away. His eyes had the sheen of unshed tears. "He'd better be treating you right."

"He is. I love you, Dad."

He pulled her close again and whispered, "Love you back, sunshine. So much."

Dinner at The Association lived up to the hype. The place was all dark wood, beamed ceilings, leather furniture and Craftsman-style lamps. Wes had reserved a private dining room, just for the two of them.

The giant, fancy menu had no prices on it. The service was impeccable and Evy's steak melted on her tongue. They lingered over an excellent bottle of Cabernet Sauvignon and she ate every bite of her strawberry-and-chocolate crumble dessert.

As they drove to the Flying A, her heart felt like it was made of helium, lighter than air. The mountains in the distance reached toward the endless, starry Montana sky. Her stomach swooshed with nerves. She seesawed between bliss and edgy anticipation.

He reached across the console, took her hand and brought it to his lips. Shivers whispered down her spine just at the feel of his mouth on her skin. "You're quiet," he said, as he twined their fingers together.

She pulled their joined hands into her lap. It felt good, right, to be here beside him, her fingers woven with his. "Just thinking…"

"About…?"

Love, Wes. I think I'm in love with you.

She swallowed. Hard. And she tried to summon all the usual denials, that he didn't want her love or anyone's. That she wasn't ready for love, that the timing was all wrong.

But her denials were only lies, pure and simple.

And she was tired of lying. The truth had finally found her. And it would not be denied.

I love you, Weston Abernathy. I love you so much...

She opened her mouth to say it aloud—but no. It really was too soon.

She'd just now accepted the truth herself.

And he *didn't* accept it.

He *wouldn't* accept it.

Especially not while he was driving, for crying out loud. If she hit him with that news right now, they would end up in a ditch.

"That dessert," she lied, and put on a bright smile. "It was amazing."

At the cabin, he took her overnight bag from the back seat and went around to open her door. They strolled up the walk and onto the porch hand in hand.

She pulled him back before they went inside. "Where's Archie?"

"With Susanna and Dean for the night."

"It's a beautiful night. Let's sit out here for a while."

"Sure." He took her in his arms and kissed her, a long, deep, delicious kiss. "I can't believe you're here for the whole night. Just you and me. We can make all the noise we want."

"I know, right?" She kissed him again. "We can relax, do whatever comes naturally."

He made a low sound of agreement. "We can take our time."

"Not sneak around and have to constantly remind each other to keep it down."

"Exactly." He gestured at the waiting Adirondack chairs. "Have a seat. Stare up at that sliver of moon. Want a drink or some coffee?"

"Nothing. Just you."

"Hold that thought." He went inside with her suitcase. A moment later, he settled into the chair beside her. Hers wasn't close enough for his liking. Reaching over, he grabbed the chair arm and pulled her toward him. Her chair skittered on the porch boards until it met his. "Kiss me."

She didn't have to be told twice. They kissed and then kissed some more.

Both of them were grinning when they sat back in their chairs and stared out at the clear night sky.

"Evy…" He leaned in to kiss her yet again and she leaned to meet him—and right then, it happened.

She felt her heart taking charge, slipping the bonds of her good sense. With a sharp intake of breath, she froze before their lips could touch.

He asked in a teasing tone, "Change your mind?"

"Uh-uh. Never. My mind is made up."

"Yeah? About what?"

"You, Weston." Her heart seemed to expand in her chest. It pressed against her rib cage, aching with emotion, wanting only to get closer to him. "Oh, Wes." And the truth got away from her. "I love you. I never really thought I would say that to any man again—or if I did, not for a long, long time. But now I know you, and you are everything I ever dreamed of. You are the man for me. I love you with all my heart. I…" She lost her train of thought.

Because he didn't look happy. He looked…far away. His eyes had gone flat, his mouth curving down.

And then he sank back to his own chair.

She felt frozen in place, leaning toward him, waiting for…

What?

His focus was not on her. He stared out somewhere past his pickup, beyond the pasture fence and the rolling field of yellowed grass, past the next fence over and the shadowed shape of the weathered barn way out there under the star-thick sky.

One moment he was right here, all hers.

And the next, he was miles from here. Lost out there in the dark of night.

Finally, she asked in small voice, "So, um… More information than you needed, huh?"

He turned to her. "Evy…" It was awful, the way

he said her name. Reluctant. Uncomfortable. With regret and self-reproach.

She drew in a slow, shaky breath. "Whatever it is, would you please just go ahead and say it?"

"It's only that I…" The moment stretched so thin she could hear it scream in agony. "I thought you understood. We talked about it. We agreed that we'd get to know each other, have fun together and that's all. I've tried to stick to the plan. When it started to feel more serious, I tried to walk away, tried to *stay* away…" Slowly, he shook his head, his gaze still focused on the dark shadows of the mountains straining toward the indigo sky. "But then you came after me. There you were last Sunday, waiting for me right here on my front porch. You said you weren't looking for love and I said I wasn't, either." He met her eyes again and accused, "You said if the time came that you felt differently, you would tell me."

"Wait. Wes, I…"

"You what?" He waited for her answer. When she was silent to long, he muttered, "Just say it."

"I, um, well, I guess this is it. I *am* telling you." *And clearly, I shouldn't have.* An apology almost popped out of her mouth.

But apologize for loving him? That would just be wrong. And boy, did she feel like a complete fool now. Had it only been a week since she'd tracked him down right here on this porch and asked to try again?

A week? Surely not. At the moment it felt like she'd loved him forever.

But really, it *had* all happened so quickly. He'd been painfully clear where he stood on this issue. She was the one trying to change the rules.

She needed to slow down, dial it back. "Okay, then. Let me try to understand what you're telling me. Are you saying that you need more time? That I'm pushing too fast?" A foolish whinny of nervous laughter escaped her. She winced at the sound. "Because if you are, well, I understand. I'm not asking you to feel what I feel, Wes. Truly, I'm not. I'm just letting you know that you're, um, so important to me. That you're in my heart."

He turned away from her again and stared into the night out there beyond the glow of the porchlight, his expression unreadable.

And then he seemed to shake himself. "Evy, you are amazing. I'm wild about you, but…"

Oh, dear, sweet Lord. This was not going well. "But?"

"But I can never give you what I don't have in me."

"What you, um…" She had a million desperate questions, all starting with *why?* And continuing with *why not?* "What you don't have in you. What does that mean?"

He scoffed. "Stuff happens in life, okay? People get messed over."

"You mean *you* got messed over by that woman named Belinda?"

"Yeah, she messed me over. And I'm never going there again."

"But, Wes. I'm not her."

"Of course you're not. And I'm not the man for you. I never will be. I've seen the writing on the wall. I know who I am. I know what I'm capable of. Love and all that, it's just not for me."

"So you're saying that you don't *believe* in love?"

"I just think it's a crapshoot and I'm no damn good at it. I just don't want to play."

"You're honestly telling me that you see love as a game?"

"No. I want to be free, okay? I don't want to make someone unhappy. I don't want to be screwed over. I don't want to go there at all."

"So you, um, want to be free—yet you're figuring out ways to be with me every chance you get? Wes, you don't act like some player, you really don't. You act like a guy who wants just what I want. The right person to be with. Someone to count on. Someone who laughs at the same things you do, someone strong and true to stand beside you. Someone to make the good times better and the bad times bearable."

"You're wrong. That's not what I want. That's not who I am."

"Weston, you *are* capable of loving me, of going forward in life with me. You've been showing me how very capable you are every single day."

He shut his eyes, shook his head. "No. Uh-uh. I'm not. I'm really not. You need to take my word for it."

"But I think you're lying—not to me, to yourself."

He got up. Stepping to the porch rail, he stared out at the night. "Look. I'm the bad guy here. I knew from the beginning what kind of woman you are."

She rose on shaky legs and went to stand beside him. "What do you mean, what *kind* of woman?"

Reluctantly, he faced her. "The true kind. The *let's build a life together* kind. I should have stayed away, I tried to stay away. For months and months, I tried. But there's something about you that gets to me. And now you want more because that's who you are."

"Wes. I didn't ask you for more."

"But you *want* more."

She almost denied that. But what good would lying do? "Eventually, yes. I do hope for more. But

I'm not demanding it. Right now, all I said is that I love you. I'm not asking you to say it back."

"Well, you *should* be asking me. Because you need to know the truth. Evy, this, what we have now… That's as far as things go with me. I've been telling myself lies just to be with you longer, fooling myself that we understood each other, that we both agreed it was just for fun, just for a while."

She searched his face. "It's so strange. I've known that I love you for a while now. But every time I thought it, I told myself it wasn't true. I denied what's in my heart. And now, tonight, it just popped out of my mouth anyway. I swear I wasn't going to say it. I really wasn't." She hard-swallowed. "But you know, I think I needed to say it. I needed to let you know."

"Aw, Evy…" He looked so tired now, just completely wrung out.

"I need you to tell me honestly. What do you want, Wes?"

"I want you. I want you so bad."

"Well, then. You have me. You don't have to promise me anything. Just stop pushing me away."

"You don't get it." His voice was flat, his eyes hard.

"You're right. I don't."

"I need to take you home. This can't go on, with us. Evy, it's over. We're done."

All the air had left her lungs. "So, then." It came out in an anguished whisper. She dragged in a breath. "Um. You're sure?" She felt empty. Bereft. Completely deflated, a party balloon with all the air let out, abandoned on the ground, trying really hard not to wonder what was wrong with her that she'd somehow managed to choose the wrong man—twice.

"Evy, damn it. Don't look at me like that."

"Like what?"

"Like I broke your heart."

"Yeah, well. That's how I feel right now. Like you broke my heart."

"No…" He started to reach for her.

"Don't." She put up both hands and he fell back a step.

It hurt. It hurt so bad. She really hadn't expected a promise of forever from him—not tonight, maybe not ever. But she *had* believed he would at least be open to the *idea* of loving her, that he would be willing to give love a chance.

Wrong.

He was not open nor was he willing. And she had to accept the hard truth here.

He hadn't said *not now*. He'd said *never*. He'd said it was over. He wanted to take her home.

Loving him was only a fantasy. And she needed to face reality.

He was not the man for her.

She drew herself up tall. "All right, then. We're done. Please take me home."

Chapter Ten

During the drive into Bronco Valley, Evy kept her mouth shut. Really, what more was there to say? Weston had the good grace to keep quiet, too.

At her house, he swung his door open. Before he could lower his boots to the ground, she said, "Please. Stay right where you are."

"Damn it, Evy—"

"I really don't want you to walk me to the door."

With a shake of his head, he pulled his door closed.

She got out, grabbed her overnight bag from the back seat and marched up the walk. He didn't drive away until she'd let herself inside.

And she didn't let herself cry until she was safely in her own room with the door shut.

Life went on.

The next day, Evy got up at seven and made breakfast for her dad and her little girl.

"French toast with strawberries and whipped cream!" Lola clapped her hands at the sight.

Owen said gently, "I didn't hear you come in this morning."

"Change of plans. I was home before eleven. I tried to be really quiet."

He looked at her with love and sympathy. How was it he could always read her so easily? "Ah, sunshine…"

"Sometimes things just don't work out." She pulled out his chair. "Now you sit down," she briskly commanded. "I'll get you some coffee."

He took the chair and spread his napkin in his lap. "Well. This looks delicious."

After breakfast, she cleaned up the kitchen and then went ahead and cleaned the bathrooms, too. Lola helped. Evy gave her a Swiffer hand duster and she dusted her heart out, humming as she worked. Watching her daughter flicking that Swiffer around, Evy smiled for the first time since last night on the porch at Weston's cabin.

Once again, she'd gotten it all wrong with a man.

But she had the sweetest little girl in the world and the best dad ever in her corner. Plus, her dream of creating Cimarron Rose was actually coming true.

For at least the next ten minutes, she felt better about everything.

After lunch, she drove over to Commercial Street to work at the store for a couple of hours. The remodel crew wasn't on-site today. That should have made it easier for her to concentrate on what needed doing.

But it didn't. Her spirits sagged. Thoughts of last night kept dragging her down. She just didn't feel like trying to crawl out of the miserable emotional hole she'd tumbled into. She was about to give it up for the day, go home and decide what to cook for dinner, when Shari Lormand tapped on the shop door.

As a rule, Evy adored Shari. Shari always kept things upbeat. She could put a positive spin on practically anything. Right now, though, Evy had zero interest in a positive spin. She just wanted to be left alone.

But it was too late to slip out of sight. Shari had already seen her. Plus, no way could Evy blow off a friend.

She put on a smile and let Shari in. They shared a hello hug.

"I had a little time to myself," Shari said. "We

haven't had a moment to talk in a while, but I did hear that you'd leased a great storefront in Valley Center next door to Sadie's Holiday House. Congratulations!"

"Thank you. As you can see, we're just getting started."

"Hey." Shari caught her hand. "Hold on a minute." She searched Evy's face. "You okay? What's going on?"

Evy let out a moan. "Just, you know, life."

Shari did know. She knew too well. "It's that charmer, Weston Abernathy, right?"

"Yeah," Evy confessed. "It didn't work out."

"Wait. Last time we talked about this, you were reluctant to get anything going with him."

"I was, yes."

"But you...took a chance on him, after all?"

"Yeah. Yeah, I did."

"And...?"

"We were friends and then we were more than friends. For a while, things really heated up between us—twice, that happened. We grew close. He walked away. I went after him and we worked it out. For a week, it was so good between us. Then last night, I said I loved him—and he said he would never love me back. He said that it was over."

"Oh, no..."

"Oh, yes." Evy tried to put on a smile. "So that's the end of that."

"Come here." Shari pulled her over to the folding table she'd been using as a temporary desk. "Sit." Evy dropped into the chair in front of her laptop. Shari took the other chair. "Talk. Tell me everything."

"I just did. It was good until it wasn't, both times—and, Shari, I really did try to talk it out with him. I told him honestly how I felt and I tried to understand what's going on with him. He was engaged once and she hurt him. It was a bad breakup—bad enough that he says he's not willing to try again with me."

"But surely he must see that you're a completely different person than the woman who broke his heart."

"I do think he sees that. But he still won't give it a chance with me. He was very clear that nothing would change his mind. He said I was the kind of woman who wants to build a life with a man and he will never be that man."

"He broke it off both times, then?"

"The first time, it was all him. Last night, well, I guess you could say we both agreed that it wasn't going to work."

"How do you feel about him right now?"

"Furious. Sad. I know I did the right thing to say goodbye—and I miss him so much."

"You love him."

"Ugh."

Shari took Evy's hand and gave it a squeeze. "I'll take that as a yes. And I'm predicting that, in the end, he won't be able to stay away."

Evy let out a burst of bitter laughter. "Too bad. It's over. I'm not going there again. I feel like a yo-yo. And now he's told me right to my face that he's never going to love me. I don't need that. I really don't."

"Of course you don't." Shari scooted her chair closer and wrapped an arm around Evy's shoulders. "But I'm willing to bet that when he comes back around, he'll be singing a whole different tune."

Evy sighed. "You're the best. I love how you look on the bright side, how you truly want me to be happy. But you hardly know Wes." She sank back to her own chair. "Twice, he's proven to me that no matter how great things are with us, he could bolt at any time. Hope and a positive attitude go a long way. But all the positive thoughts in the world can't turn a player into a stayer."

With a sad sigh, Shari readjusted her glasses on the bridge of her nose. "You're right. About all of it, including that I don't know Weston Abernathy except to say hi. I do know you, though. You're strong and smart and very perceptive. You're a catch. And if you're in love with him, well, he may not be the man you deserve. Not yet. But I'm betting he's got real potential."

"Maybe so. It's still over, though. And I honestly don't believe he'll be coming back to beg me for one more chance—and now, can we change the subject please?"

Shari almost looked dejected. "I think I need a hug."

"Good. So do I."

They reached out at the same time. When they pulled apart, Shari suggested, "You know, I keep meaning to try Bean & Biscotti. Buy you a coffee?"

Evy gave her friend a reluctant smile. "I would love a coffee."

They ran across the street together and had iced cappuccinos. Shari talked about her plans to expand the kids' programs at the library and Evy agreed to help out any way she could.

After Shari left, Evy realized she did feel a little better about her life and the choices she'd made. Even though her heart felt battered and bruised right now, she *had* made progress in love.

Chad had dazzled her. He'd swept her off her feet and she'd felt like a princess—for a while. Then she'd gotten pregnant and things had gotten too real, too fast. But because of Chad, she had Lola. And that made her grateful for her time with him.

As for Wes…

He was far from perfect and she'd known that from the start. But Shari was right. He was a better man than he believed himself to be, a man who would do just about anything for someone he cared about. He'd left her happier with her life than she'd been before she loved him, more confident in her own capabilities, more certain that she would make a good future for herself and for her little girl.

She would try to focus on the good Wes had done. On how he'd dragged her out of her comfort zone and into making her business dream a reality. She would remind herself how much she'd loved every moment she'd had with him—even the painful encounters with him had been honest, at least. He'd never lied to her and she had been up-front in demanding what she wanted from him.

When the pain of his rejection finally faded, she felt certain that she would remember him without bitterness.

But then at dinner that night, Lola ate a bite of her hamburger steak and announced, "Mommy, I want to call Weston tonight, and say hi. And then I want to go out to the ranch on Sunday like we always do. I want to see Archie, go swimming in the creek and get a ride on Babycakes."

At the other end of the table, Evy's dad looked slightly stricken. She'd yet to talk to him about the Weston situation, but he knew her so well. He'd already figured out that she and Wes were done. As for Lola, Evy had hoped to have a day or two at least to come up with appropriate answers when her little girl started asking where Weston had gone.

Well, so much for what she'd hoped.

Evy set down her fork. She sent her dad a sad smile and put the truth out there. "Lolly, I'm so sorry, but we're not going to be spending time with Weston anymore."

Lola set her fork down, too. It clattered against the rim of her plate. "Why not?"

Evy wanted to bop herself on the head with her water glass. It had been way too easy to let Wes into her life. For her daughter's sake if nothing else, she shouldn't have let things go so far, so fast. "For a little while, Weston was my boyfriend, but he's not anymore. And that means he won't be coming to visit us and we won't be going out to the ranch."

"But I want to see him and Archie and Babycakes."

"I know you do. I'm afraid you can't, though."

"But Weston will miss us if we're not there."

Don't mess this up any more than you already have. Keep it simple, she reminded herself. *Don't overexplain. Let her tell you how she feels, let her get it out*. "He understands that we won't be visiting the ranch anymore. He will be fine, I promise you."

"But I'll miss him if I don't get to see him."

"Yes, I know you will, honey. I'll miss him, too."

"Then we need to go see him."

"No, Lolly. We are not going to go see him."

Lola's lip quivered now. Tears rose in her eyes. "I don't like this, Mommy. I want to see Weston!"

"I'm sorry, Lolly. I really am. So, so sorry."

"Mommy…" She sniffled and the tears spilled over. A flood of them.

Evy pushed back her chair and held out her arms. She fully expected her daughter to shout *No!* and refuse to be comforted.

But Lola reached out her arms, too, and Evy scooped her close. "We'll be back," she whispered to her dad as Lola sobbed on her shoulder.

Owen looked almost as wrecked as Evy felt. "Take your time."

Evy carried her sobbing daughter down the hall. In Lola's room, she sat in the old rocker in the corner with her little girl in her lap and rocked gently as Lola cried like her heart would break.

Between sobs, Lola insisted, "I miss Babycakes! I miss Weston! I want to see Archie, I do. I miss them so much!"

The storm of weeping wore her out. She didn't object when Evy helped her into her pajamas an hour before her usual bedtime. In the bathroom, Lola sagged against the sink as she brushed her teeth.

"Come on, now." Evy led her back to her room and tucked her in.

Lola went out like a light with Tina curled into a ball beside her.

For a little while, Evy just stood by the bed, wanting what all mothers want—that her child would never have to suffer loss or loneliness. She hated that tonight she'd been the cause of her little girl's anguished tears. And she dreaded more sharply than ever the day when Lola started asking where her daddy was. So far, Lolly had Evy and her pop-pop and Dotty, loving adults who thought the sun rose and set on her. The issue hadn't come up. But it would.

Life was so messy. And sometimes, kids had to learn hard things much too soon.

When she felt reasonably certain that Lola wouldn't wake suddenly and start crying again, Evy tiptoed to the door. Slipping silently into the hall, she wandered out to the front room, where her dad sat on the long sofa under the picture window watching a baseball game on his big-screen TV.

Her dad pointed the remote at the screen and the TV went dark. "How's she doing?"

"She's asleep. I'm hoping she'll feel better in the morning."

He patted the spot next to him on the sofa. Evy went and sat beside him. When he hooked his big arm around her, she let herself lean on him. "How about you, sweetheart?" He smoothed a hand down her hair. "Will you be all right?"

She hitched up a shoulder in a weary shrug. "I'll be okay. Eventually. But still. It hurts. I love him, Dad. I do."

Her dad gave her a squeeze. "He's a damn fool to walk away from my girl."

"I could not agree with you more."

Wes had thought it was bad when Belinda walked out on him.

Losing Evy was worse.

So much worse.

At least with Belinda, he'd been the wounded party. But now he was the bad guy. He'd done everything wrong—for Evy, for Lola, for his own messed-up self. He not only missed Evy more than he'd ever missed Belinda, but losing Evy had been his own damn fault.

He never should have let himself get so close to her. He should have played it cool and easy the way he'd been doing for more than ten years—except who did he think he was kidding?

There was no playing it cool and easy for him when it came to Evy. And that meant he should never have pursued her in the first place. He should have locked himself down, should have listened to Garrett and Maddox, respected the challenges she faced as a young, single mother, accepted his own unwillingness to be the good, steady man she deserved—and stayed the hell away from her.

Instead, he just couldn't leave her be. He'd burned so hot for her, he'd broken all his own rules, twisted everything up, told himself—and her— that it was just for fun and just for now, at the same time as he'd wormed his way into her everyday life, angled to spend every minute he could with her, butted in to help her achieve her dreams, pushed her to let him get to know her dad and her little girl.

He'd hurt her, exactly as Garrett and Maddox had predicted he would. He'd hurt her and now it was over.

And all he could think about was how much he missed her. He couldn't stop wondering how she was doing, what Lola was up to and whether or not Owen would show up on his doorstep ready to kick his ass.

Not that Wes would blame Owen for wanting to go a few rounds. Wes deserved a good whupping. If Owen came after him, Wes would spread his arms wide, say, "Have at it, man. Do your worst," and then he would stand there and take it.

Yeah, he was a wreck, all right. Sunday night, when he got home alone after dropping her off at her dad's for the last time, he didn't sleep a wink.

Monday, he kept to himself. He and Archie went out good and early. Working alone, he did what needed doing on the land—pulling a half-drowned calf from a pond, clearing weeds from a stagnant ditch—tasks he'd mastered before he'd even hit his teens. He took his phone with him. He would answer it if it looked like something important and then quickly get rid of whoever had contacted him. Each beep, every ring—they got his heart racing, thinking it might be Evy.

He knew damn well she wouldn't be calling to beg him to try again strictly for now and strictly for fun. All that was over. He'd said they were through and she hadn't argued. She'd made up her mind about him, and a woman like Evy stuck to her guns.

By Monday evening, he was a straight-up walking disaster, miserable to the core.

His mom stopped by the cabin as he was trying to decide what to fix for dinner. She asked him if he was okay. He assured her he was fine and sent her on her way.

As he stood on the porch watching her drive off, Archie gave a plaintive little whine.

He looked down at the dog. "What is it, boy?"

The pup stared up at him with anxious eyes.

"I'm fine," he said.

Archie didn't seem convinced.

Because Wes wasn't fine. He missed Evy, missed her so bad.

Less than twenty-four hours had passed since he left her at her father's house and already, he was starting to get it, starting to understand that he'd been lying to himself about what Evy was to him, kidding himself that he would be fine when it was over between them. Fact was, he had way too much false pride and he'd never let go of it. And now, because of a promise he'd made to himself when he was twenty-two years old, he'd lost the best thing that had ever happened to him.

He hated the cabin now. He'd been so happy there, with her and Lola.

Now it was just an empty shell of logs and chinking. It served only to remind him that she wasn't here anymore. He kept thinking he smelled roses and sugar cookies. The scent of her lurked in the kitchen, in his bedroom, waiting to seep from every corner and fill his head with sweetness and longing.

He hardly knew what to do with himself. He ate a sandwich for dinner and fell into bed, exhausted. Sleep should have rolled right over him. After all, he'd worked like a demon all day.

But all he did was stare wide-awake into the darkness, despising himself, wondering what in hell was wrong with him, to let Evy get away, to lose her for no reason, really—just the old reasons that had once seemed so important to him, reasons that were only crappy excuses not to step up and claim his woman, not to be the man she needed him to be.

Tuesday morning at the ass-crack of dawn, he and Archie headed out again. He fixed fences, groomed horses and baled hay.

Every time he turned around, there was Archie, watching him. Like a four-legged ICU nurse with a terminal patient, ready to leap into action when all the machines started beeping and it was time to bring on the defibrillators and perform CPR, Archie kept close.

That evening, Maddox showed up. Wes was sprawled in one of the porch chairs with Archie beside him. He'd been thinking he probably ought to go see about fixing some food, but then, he didn't really care if he ate or not.

"Wes, my man!" Maddox called as he climbed from his pickup. "Get your ass up out of that chair. Let's head into town, drink some beer, play some pool."

"Sorry, Maddox. Not in the mood."

Maddox rounded the bed of his pickup and

mounted the steps. "You look like someone stole your horse. What's up?"

"None of your business."

"Whoa. You're giving me attitude? Wait. Let me guess. It's all about a very pretty woman with green eyes and black hair. What the hell, buddy? You know better than this."

"I don't want to talk about it."

Maddox took off his black hat and resettled it back on his head. "The way you look right now, I see no choice but to give it to you straight. It's too late for you. You're doomed."

"Tell me about it."

"I heard that you and Evy got back together."

"For a while, yeah."

"And now you're on the outs again?"

"I don't want to talk about it, Maddox."

"Whatever you say, man." Maddox turned, went back down the steps and around the rear of his pickup to the driver's-side door. He slapped a hand on the roof of the cab. "Maybe you ought to rethink things a little. You look bad. Just go work it out with her. Take her flowers. Whatever you did, tell the woman you're sorry."

"Weren't you the one who said to leave Evy alone?"

"Yeah. But I can see that's not working for you. Maybe you should just go after her. Work it out."

Wes said nothing. Really, what the hell was there to say?

Maddox slapped the roof of the cab again. "Look. What can I do? What do you need?"

"Nothing. I mean it. I'm fine."

"You don't look fine."

Wes kept his mouth shut.

Maddox put up both hands. "All right. You call if you need anything. I'm out of here. Later, man." Wes gave him a wave. Maddox climbed back in the pickup and kicked up a cloud of dust driving away.

The rest of the evening crawled by and the night was never-ending. Same as Sunday and Monday night, he hardly slept a wink.

Wednesday morning good and early, he dragged himself from his bed, drank half a pot of coffee and headed out to fix downed fences.

By early afternoon, he was a few miles from the cabin, working his way along a line of busted-through fence. He'd set his mind to staying strictly focused on the job at hand. Thus, for a little while at least, he could keep thoughts of his own pig-headed idiocy at bay.

On his knees at the fence, he was splicing a line of broken wire. As for Archie, last time Wes had glanced over his shoulder, the pup had looked reasonably content lying in the grass a few feet behind him.

Wes had just finished looping the broken wire. He was rolling out a fresh length for the repair when the pup let out a low growl of warning.

Wes whipped his head around to see Archie on his feet, hackles raised. The dog barked a stronger warning—and Wes spotted the threat.

A black bear raced toward them.

"Stay!" Wes shouted as he shot to his feet and went for the handgun holstered at his hip.

Archie, always obedient until now, ignored Wes's command and took off like a shot to meet the charging bear. About then, in the diminishing space between the dog and the bear, Wes spotted two cubs. He hesitated the fraction of an instant it took for the mama bear to lurch to a stop and swing out one giant paw.

With a startled cry, Archie went flying. The mama bear, already turning away, nosed the nearest cub to get a move on. The three lumbered off through the grass.

His heartbeat roaring in his ears, Wes let them go. He didn't have it in him to kill a mama with cubs—not when the damage was already done, the threat in retreat.

As for the damage…

Archie lay sprawled on his side several feet away. He wasn't moving.

Wes sucked in a slow breath. His heart lurching

now, his feet suddenly heavy as twin slabs of concrete, he approached the motionless dog.

"Archie…" He dropped to his knees. "Damn it, Arch—"

The pup didn't respond.

Wes swiped the sudden moisture from his eyes with the back of his leather glove. "Just had to save my sorry ass, didn't you, boy?"

Archie couldn't hear him. The blow—or maybe the fall—had knocked the pup out cold. Wes put two fingers to the side of his neck.

Archie's big heart was still beating. Lightly, he laid a hand to Archie's ribs and felt steady movement beneath his palm.

Still breathing.

Wes debated. Was it unsafe to move him? Should he call Bronco Heights Animal Hospital and ask for Felix Sanchez? The large-animal veterinarian took care of stock for all the local ranches. How long would it take for Felix to get here?

Too long.

"It's okay, boy. You're going to be okay." He knew Archie couldn't hear him. Still, he chanted the words like a mantra as he started to lift him, falling silent when he felt the sticky warmth of blood on Archie's underside. "What the…?"

By feel, he identified the source of the injury. A sharp rock poked up through the grass.

Not only knocked out cold, but cut up—and pretty bad, too.

Wes tore off his shirt to bandage the wound. Carefully lifting the limp puppy, Wes eased the shirt beneath him, pausing to press the jagged edges of the gash together as best he could while his fingers slid around in way too much blood.

Finally, he joined the shirtsleeves in a knot to secure the makeshift bandage in place. It wouldn't stay that way if Archie woke up and started moving around.

Sadly, he didn't know which to wish for—that Archie stay knocked out, or that he come to right now. Extended unconsciousness couldn't be good. But if he woke up, he would move around and disturb his injury.

Very gently, Wes gathered the limp pup into his arms and headed for his truck.

Chapter Eleven

Weston called Bronco Heights Animal Hospital from the truck. Felix Sanchez just happened to be the vet on duty. Wes felt a faint surge of relief when the receptionist put Felix on the line.

Intense and always serious, Felix was a good man and a fine veterinarian. He'd saved the day more than once for the animals on the Flying A. The vet said he would ready an exam room and meet him in the parking lot with a gurney.

The ride to town went by in a blur. Wes's pulse pounded in his ears as he bounced over ruts. The dirt road did not make for a smooth ride. He muttered a string of profanities under his breath as he tried to balance getting there fast with avoiding potholes and gullies.

The ride smoothed out once he reached the main road into town, but every time he glanced over the seat at the unconscious pup all covered in blood, his heart sank again.

Finally, he turned into the veterinary hospital parking lot where Felix and an assistant waited. As he pulled to a stop, he heard a whine from the back seat. His heart lurched at the sound.

"Hey there," he said over the seat. "You're okay, boy. You're going to be just fine…"

Wes stood back, sick with worry, as Felix and his assistant carefully transferred Archie to the dog-sized gurney and got a blood drip going. Archie whimpered in distress, but he didn't struggle much.

Inside, Wes followed the gurney into the exam room. Archie licked his fingers and looked at him through those big trusting eyes as Wes explained what had happened and Felix said what Wes already knew—that Archie's wound would require surgery.

The vet arched a thick, dark brown eyebrow at Wes's bare chest. "You need a shirt?"

"Yeah. If you've got a spare, I sure would appreciate it."

"No problem." Felix sent the assistant off to get his spare shirt from behind the door in his office.

The woman returned a few minutes later with a blue button-up.

After washing up in the men's room as best he could, Wes put on the borrowed shirt and took a chair in the waiting area. Each minute that went by felt like an hour. Finally, one of the women behind the front counter led him into the back again. He got to see Archie, who was still conked out from the anesthesia. The pup looked peaceful, at least. He was already wearing one of those cone collars.

Felix explained, "The surgery went well. He's breathing normally and should recover just fine. We're treating him with an antibiotic to stave off possible infection and a strong painkiller through the drip. He'll be out for a while."

"Thank you." Wes spoke quietly, though inside he was raging. He should've kept a closer eye on the pup. He should've turned around sooner, drawn his pistol faster...

Felix nodded. "I'm just happy to be able to say that he'll pull through."

"Thank God."

"He looks like one of the famous Maggie's pups."

"He is. And he's a great guy. Best damn dog ever."

"Sorry, but he should stay here for a couple of days at least. We need to keep a close eye on him."

"Okay. How much pain will he be in when he wakes up?"

"We'll manage that with medication, keep him comfortable, I promise you."

"Good." Wes didn't want to leave him.

Felix must have figured out what Wes was thinking. "Sorry. You can't stay with him."

Reluctantly, Wes nodded. "I guess I knew that. Is there someone here at night?"

Felix assured him that there would be a tech on duty at all times. "Archie will be closely watched, especially this first night. Once he wakes up, the E-collar will keep him from licking or tearing off his bandages."

Wes thanked Felix again, and then moved on to the front desk to settle up for now.

Outside in the parking lot, a lady with a fat, fluffy cat in her arms looked at him kind of funny. Maybe it was the dazed expression on his face, or possibly the blood all over his faded work jeans.

He climbed in his truck and just sat there behind the wheel, not sure what to do with himself next.

A shower and a change of clothes might help.

He drove home on autopilot. At the Flying A, he took off the shirt Felix had loaned him. Then he set to work mopping up the blood in the back seat.

The seat itself was black and the thick mats on the floor hosed right off. When he was finished, the back seat looked almost as good as new—a lot better than Archie had looked back at the animal hospital, all wrapped up in bandages, hooked to an IV and wearing a plastic cone around his neck. How much blood had the poor guy lost, anyway?

Probably better not to let himself think about that, to focus on the fact that Felix was an excellent vet who had seemed confident that Archie would pull through just fine.

By the time Wes had showered, put on clean clothes and washed Felix's shirt, it was after five.

He should eat. But he didn't feel hungry. His brain wouldn't move out of crisis mode. He kept thinking of Archie getting all busted up protecting him, of Evy, of the look on her face when he stomped all over her true, tender heart.

Restless, fed up with his own damn self, he climbed in his truck again, drove back out to the main road and turned toward town. With no idea where he was going or why, he just kept driving, turning one corner and then another, ending up on Commercial Street, cruising southeast until he drove past Evy's store.

She wasn't there that he could see—nobody was. The lights were off inside. He felt let down and knew he was being ridiculous.

Not to mention a creeper. He had no right to go seeking her out.

But he needed to see her, to tell her about Archie. He just…

Well, he needed to talk to her.

He really did.

He turned the next corner and the next one after that, until he found himself turning onto her street—yeah. Creeper. No doubt about it now.

A minute later, he was rolling to a stop in front of her house.

He shouldn't be here. He had no right to be here—and yet he leaned on his door and got out. He marched up the walk, mounted the front steps and knocked on the door with no clue of what to say to her. There really was no excuse for his presence on her doorstep.

Owen answered.

Wes sucked in a slow, unsteady breath as he stared into the frowning face of Evy's dad. "Uh. Hi, Owen."

"You look like a long stretch of bad road," the older man said, his tone much gentler than Wes deserved. Shaking his head, Owen stepped back. "Come on in." He gestured through the open double doors to the front room. "Have a seat."

On automatic pilot now, Wes obeyed. He sat on the end of the sofa. Lola's kitten slept on the other end, curled in a ball, that heart-shaped marking dark as night against the snow-white fur above her tail.

Owen took the leather club chair. "Everlee's not here. She spent most of the day at her shop, then went to the bar early. Doug needed her to cover for him. He had errands to run or something."

"Right. What about Lola?"

"She's not here, either. She went home with one of her daycare friends. They're having a cookout in the backyard. I'm picking her up at seven." Owen settled back in the chair and looked at him expectantly.

Wes knew it was his turn to talk. Too bad he didn't have a single coherent thing to say.

Owen prompted, "Talk to me, Wes. What's going on?"

"I…" For a moment, he knew he would not find another word in his brain to push out his mouth. But then he heard himself say, "Archie took on a mama bear today out at the Flying A. He was protecting me. He almost got killed in the process."

"Whoa. But he's okay?"

"He will be, yeah. The vet says he'll make a full recovery."

"Damn. That's a relief—and what about you, Wes? You could have been torn to pieces."

"I'm fine. Thanks to Archie."

"Well, then. Count your blessings, as they say."

"Right." A silence fell between them. Wes had

so much to say and no idea where to begin. "Listen, Owen, I…" Words deserted him again.

Now Evy's dad was eyeing him warily. "I'm listening."

Wes sat forward. "Look, I know I messed up with Evy. I messed up so bad. And I miss her. It's been three days since I screwed everything up. It feels like a century. I'm hopeless. Can't sleep, can't eat. I just I want to make it right. But I don't know if there's any way to do that. I don't even know if I deserve a chance to make it right." For a moment, Wes thought he saw sympathy in Owen's eyes.

But then the older man said, deadpan, "You probably don't."

Wes grunted. "You're probably right."

Owen made a thoughtful sound. "Then again, screwing up is part of life. And frankly, Wes, we might as well be straight with each other. We both know you're in love with my daughter."

What could he say to that—except the truth? "You're right. I love Evy so much it hurts. I thought I was in love once before. I realize now I didn't even know the meaning of the word back then."

"So you broke my daughter's heart because some other woman screwed you over, is that what you're telling me?" Owen's words were tough, but his voice was strangely gentle.

"When you put it that way, it sounds pretty stupid."

"Yes, it does. Wes, we both know it's not my Everlee's fault what some other woman did."

"I do know that. I never blamed Evy."

"Nonetheless, you went and stomped on her heart."

"Like I said, I messed up. I need to make it right, Owen."

Evy's dad said nothing for several very long seconds. Finally, he leaned forward and braced his beefy forearms on his spread knees. "I ought to punch your lights out."

Wes just shrugged. After all, he agreed. "You want to take it to the backyard, maybe? Avoid getting blood on the furniture?"

Owen stared at him some more, scowling. "As it turns out, I'm feeling generous today. And I don't really need to beat you up. I can see you're doing a pretty good job of that yourself. I want you and Everlee to make it work together. I think you're a good man. But if you give her the runaround again…"

"I won't, Owen. I swear to you."

"All right. I'll take you at your word. Just don't disappoint me."

"I won't. One chance to fix what I broke. That's all I need. I'll never need another one. I've messed up and I know it. But I've faced the truth now. There's no going back. Evy's the one for me and all I want to do is make it right between us."

Evy's phone vibrated in her pocket. She checked, saw it was her dad and slipped into the break room to call him back.

"Hi, sweetheart. Just thought you should know that Weston was here at the house. He wants to see you."

Her heart was suddenly racing, but she made herself ask calmly, "About what?"

"Claims he made a big mistake letting you go. I believe him. He wants to talk to you. I'm thinking he'll be showing up there at the bar sometime tonight."

Did her racing heart skip a beat? Oh, yeah. She firmly reminded herself not to jump to conclusions. She needed to hear what he had to say before getting her hopes up. "Thanks for the heads-up."

"Always—oh, and Archie's at Bronco Heights Animal Hospital. He had a run-in with a bear."

"Oh, no!"

"Yeah. He's pretty beat up, but Weston says he's going to pull through."

"Poor Archie."

"Yeah. Now, what about you?"

"What about me?"

"Sunshine, don't play tough with your dear old dad. I've got your number. Your tender heart always gives you away."

"Dad." She put on her most self-assured tone. "Don't worry about me please. I'll be fine."

"You sure you don't need your old man to back you up? I can get Dotty to pick up Lola and look after her for a while."

Her heart warmed. Owen Roberts always had her back. "I love you, Dad. And I can deal with Weston, no problem."

"I figured you would say that. But remember. All you have to do is call," he said gruffly. "I'm there."

She thanked him and went back to work.

Doug returned at eight. The place filled up. Wes never showed and Evy did her best to keep her mind on the job.

By 2:30 a.m. Thursday morning, all she wanted was a hot bath followed by her own comfy bed. In the break room, she put her apron in her locker, stuffed her tips into her purse and anchored the strap on her shoulder.

"'Night, Doug," she said as she headed for the outside door.

"'Night, Everlee. Thanks again for coming in early."

"Happy to help." She went out into the cool, quiet night feeling glad that she'd driven her car. It was just a few blocks to the house, but she'd been on her feet for way too many hours already.

She'd taken maybe two steps toward her Outback when she saw Wes's crew cab. The only other vehicle left in the lot, it was parked beneath one of the lights. She could see Wes sitting in there behind the wheel.

She was dead on her feet. Still, her heart started thumping like it would poke a hole clean through her chest.

His door opened. Boots crunched gravel. "Evy." He looked exhausted. She ached for him—and at the same time, she almost laughed. What a pair they were, facing off in Doug's parking lot in the middle of the night, both of them weary to their bones.

She drew herself up. "You okay? My dad told me about poor Archie."

"He's going to be fine. And yeah, I'm all right."

"Ah. Well, that's good." She pasted on a smile.

He asked, "Can we talk? Just for a minute?" He had his hat in his hands. A spear of longing poked right through her. He looked so sad, yet as tall and strong and handsome as ever. The light overhead picked up glints of bronze in his dark brown hair.

Resettling the strap of her bag on her shoulder, she hitched her chin a little higher. "What?"

His gaze ran over her. "You look beautiful."

She hardly knew what to say, so she said nothing, just stared right back at him, longing moving through her like a pulse.

He fiddled with the brim of his hat. "I blew it. I was scared and I screwed up. You offered me everything and I turned you down. I know I've got no right to ask, but Evy, please give me one more chance."

Her stupid heart lifted. "Why?"

"You're it for me, Evy. I've been all wrong, but I want to make things right."

She felt hope rising—and fear, too. Her heart felt so tender. She wanted to cry. "I, um. I'm really tired. It's been a long shift…"

"Later, then? Just tell me when."

"Tomorrow?"

"You got it. What time?"

"Noon."

"All right. I'll see you at noon."

She turned her back on him and started walking. At her car, she tossed her bag across the seat and slipped in behind the wheel.

He remained right where she'd left him, hat in hand, watching her as she drove away.

At home, the house was quiet. She peeked in on her dad and Lola. Sound asleep, both of them.

In the hall bathroom, she took a quick shower and then went straight to bed. She had Wes on her mind and she was a bundle of nerves about tomorrow. Still, when her head hit the pillow, she dropped right off to sleep.

She woke at a few minutes after ten, pulled on her light robe and headed for the kitchen, where she found a note from her dad letting her know that he and Dotty would drop Lola off at daycare, after which they had some shopping to do. He ended with, *Got my phone and I'll keep it close. You need me, you call me. I'll be there.*

She smiled when she read that part. When it came to fathers, she'd hit the jackpot.

At eleven, after two cups of coffee and a plate of scrambled eggs, she started to get nervous. Weston would be knocking on the door in an hour—unless he'd changed his mind. He'd seemed so sincere last night. But he had issues. And so did she. Love hadn't been easy on either of them.

Her stomach all swoopy and her cheeks feeling hot, she straightened up the kitchen and then returned to her room to get dressed.

Wes stopped to check on Archie before going to see Evy.

At Bronco Heights Animal Hospital, the lady at the desk said Felix was working on-call today. Wes gave her the blue shirt and she promised to get it to him.

Then a veterinary nurse gave him an update on Archie's progress and led him back for a visit.

Archie lay in his crate, looking miserable, all bandaged up and wearing that damn cone. But they'd taken him off the drip, at least. He lifted his head and gave a weak bump of his tail against the crate floor when Wes said his name. The nurse let him open the door and carefully scratch behind the poor guy's ears as he whispered reassurances that Archie would be coming home soon.

Before he left, he promised the pup that he would return tomorrow. Archie looked at him doubtfully and let out a sad little whine.

"He really is much better," said the nurse.

"Yeah. I see that." Wes forced a smile.

He left the hospital at a little after eleven, too soon to show up on Evy's doorstep. Yeah, he wanted to think that she would be glad to see him if he arrived early. He tried to tell himself that eagerness would gain him points toward regaining her trust.

But then again, she just might slam the door in his face for not only being a fatheaded jerk who'd turned his back on her love, but also an entitled ass, a guy completely unwilling to follow simple instructions.

Uh-uh. A man in his position needed *not* to make assumptions.

He found a coffee place and got a tall cup to go.

Then he went to Bronco Park, where he sat on a bench sipping his coffee while mentally practicing his heartfelt apology, followed by an eloquent declaration of undying love.

And okay, his declaration didn't sound all that eloquent inside his head. But he was no poet and she already knew that. He would say what was in his heart and hope that just maybe she would believe him.

At noon on the nose, he knocked on her door.

He barely had a chance to lower his arm before the door swung open and she was standing there.

Dear God, she looked good—more beautiful than ever, in faded cutoffs and a little red T-shirt, her thick black hair piled in a messy bun on top of her head, her face scrubbed clean of makeup and a mug of coffee in her hand.

"Evy. Hi."

"Hi." Her voice had a slight quaver in it. She sounded nervous. He wanted to grab her and hold her and promise her there was nothing for her to be nervous about. Stepping back, she gestured for him to take a seat in the front room. As he had yesterday when he talked to Owen, he sat on the sofa. "Want some coffee?" she asked.

"No, thanks. I'm good."

She set her mug on the low table between them

and took the club chair. "Did you get to see Archie yet today?"

"Yeah. He looks pretty miserable."

"Poor guy."

"True. He's not a happy camper, all wrapped in bandages with one of those cones around his neck. But he wagged his tail a little when he saw me. He really is better, much better."

She put her slim hand against her chest, as though to soothe her racing heart. "I'm so glad."

He stared at her. Her cheeks were pink, the silky skin of her neck all flushed with color, too. He wanted to grab her and kiss her and never, ever let her go.

But he *had* let her go and he wouldn't be getting any kisses from her until he convinced her that she was everything to him, that he would never walk away from her again. "Is your dad here?"

She pressed those soft lips together and shook her head. "He took Lola to daycare and then he and Dotty had some shopping to do."

He felt relief, that it was only the two of them in the house, that her dad wouldn't suddenly appear in the doorway just as he was declaring his undying love.

Also, that they were alone gave him hope that he hadn't completely obliterated her trust. At least she was willing to talk with him in private.

She folded her hands in her lap, looked down at them and then up at him again. "You had something you wanted to say?"

He did. So much. Too much, really. He hardly knew where to start. "Sunday night, you said that you loved me. I didn't…uh, take it well. I would like a chance to show you that I can do better."

She caught her the corner of her lip between her pretty white teeth. "You seemed really sure when you turned me down."

"I was scared, Evy. Scared to say I love you back—even though I do love you and I've been miserable every moment since I dropped you off here that night."

She sat with her knees pressed together, hands still folded tightly in her lap, her dark head tipped down again. "You love me." She said it quietly, not raising her head. He had no idea what she thought, how she felt.

"I do love you," he said with all the yearning in his heart. "So much."

"Why were you scared to tell me how you feel?"

"I got my heart broke when I was twenty-two."

"Right. You mentioned that once before, that her name was Belinda, that she dumped you."

"Until then, I always knew I would find the right girl, get married, make a family. After she messed me over, I swore I would never get serious with a woman again. I made such a fool of myself over her. It broke me, you know. I just knew I could never go there again.

"And I stuck to that plan for a lot of years—until you. Evy, I knew from the first that you were good, true, full of heart. I knew it would be wrong to go after you. I tried to stay away, but I couldn't. I should've stood up, been a better man about it, either left you the hell alone or changed my ways. Instead, I wanted to have it *both* ways. I wanted to call it casual and still get to be with you."

She sent him a sideways glance. "Hold on a minute."

"Yeah?"

"Let's go back a little."

"Okay."

"About Belinda…"

He coughed to clear the log in his throat. "Right."

"Tell me about her."

"Uh. Right now?"

She nodded. "Right now."

Talking about Belinda was the last thing he wanted to do. But he would do anything to get straight with Evy.

"I, um, met her at Texas A&M, sophomore year. She was a Dallas girl. I fell hard. And she said she felt the same. We started dating and we were inseparable. I just knew I'd found the one for me."

"So you proposed."

"Right. I popped the question at homecoming, senior year. Belinda said yes and agreed to move to Montana. I was going to build us our dream house and we would live the perfect life, together, on the Flying A."

"So, what went wrong, exactly?"

"She came to Montana at Christmas break that year, to meet the family. I had thought it was going well—until I woke up Christmas morning and she was gone. She'd left a note on her pillow that she couldn't go through with it. Belinda wrote that she was a Dallas girl through and through, that life on a Montana ranch just wasn't for her, that she missed her family already and that she and I were a bad idea. She left the ring I bought her on the nightstand."

"And that was it?" Evy had those big green eyes locked on him now. She was leaning forward, kind of hanging on his every word. He really hated telling this story, but it was worth it, if it helped her to understand why he'd screwed up so bad the other night. She prompted, "You never saw her again?"

This was the worst part. "Oh, I saw her."

"That same day, on Christmas?"

"Yeah. I managed to get a flight that afternoon and I tracked her down that night at her family's big house in Turtle Creek. She refused to speak to me. She had one of her brothers tell me to go away and stop embarrassing her. But I wouldn't give up. I climbed in her bedroom window and pleaded with her to reconsider, to give our love another chance.

"She kept telling me to go away and when I wouldn't, she sicced her brothers on me. There were three of them. It was not my finest hour. I did some damage, but they bloodied me up good and proper…"

"So you went home?"

"I did, yeah. I hadn't told the family where I was going. I'd disappeared, turned off my phone so I wouldn't see all the texts and the worried calls from my parents."

"They must have been frantic."

"Yes, they were. When I got to the Flying A, my mother cried at the sight of me. I was a mess, my face swollen up, two black eyes, my hands beat to hell."

"Oh, Wes. I'm so sorry…"

"It was a long time ago."

"But that doesn't make it any less awful."

"True. I was beat to hell. I felt like the biggest fool in Montana—but the truth is, Evy, I've held onto it for too damn long."

She gave him a trembling little smile and a tiny nod of her head. "Then what happened?"

"My dad demanded to know where I'd been,

who I'd tangled with. I gave them the short version, that Belinda and I were through, that I'd taken on her three brothers in Turtle Creek and gotten my ass whupped. My mom and dad, my brothers… they all looked at me with pity in their eyes. They tiptoed around me like I was some delicate emotional flower. And I was. I moped like a lost calf for weeks.

"Slowly, though, I stopped feeling pitiful and started getting mad."

She was nodding, her legs drawn up on the chair cushion now, arms wrapped around them, pretty chin resting on her knees. "And that's when you decided you were through with love?"

"Yep. So through. Done. Stick-a-fork-in-me finished. The way I saw it, the disaster with Belinda was proof positive that the last thing I needed in my life ever again was to fall for some woman and have her take a wrecking ball to my heart.

"From then on, I played it easy, kept things casual. I had fun and I showed the women I went out with a good time and I never, ever got serious— until you, Evy. Until now."

He sat forward, holding her gaze, willing her to believe in him again. "I know I've disappointed you. I've hurt you. I did you wrong. Because I *was* wrong, Evy. So damn wrong. I was a stubborn, hopeless fool."

Her eyes shone brighter than ever with unshed tears. "No. You were just trying to protect your heart. I can see that now. I wish you had told me this story earlier. It would have helped me to understand you better if I knew the details of what you went through."

"I should have been braver. But I wasn't. I turned you down and since then, I've been paying the price of losing the best thing that ever happened to me—you, Evy. You're the one—but I swear to you that I know what I want now. I know who I love. I love *you*, Everlee Roberts. I love you and I want you and I miss you so damn much. It's a bad ache in the center of my chest, Evy. An ache that won't go away." He rose from the sofa.

Her beautiful face lifted to him as he stood and her green eyes gleamed up at him, full of hope—and maybe the stubborn remnants of fully justified doubt.

He stepped around the coffee table, sank to his knees before her—and reached for her hand. Joy ricocheted through him when she let him take it. "I want one more chance with you. Just one, because that's all I'm going to need. One more chance to prove to you that I'm the guy for you, that we should be a family, you and me and Lola. One more chance to show you that you are and always will be everything to me."

* * *

Evy couldn't do it.

She could not hold out against the love in his eyes, could not fight the sincerity in his words.

Honestly, who did she think she was kidding? She didn't *want* to fight his love. He was her dream come true. He'd screwed up, yeah. He'd broken her heart.

But her heart was feeling just fine right now. He had told her what she needed to hear and she believed him. "I love you, too," she whispered. "The truth is, I never stopped."

He stood again and pulled her up with him. "Come here. Nice and close." His strong arms encircled her. And then he said the words she had never expected to hear. "Marry me, Evy—now, next week, whenever you're ready. We're going to be so good together, you'll see. Everything is workable, everything will be all right. As long as I have you and you have me."

She reached up, gently pressed two fingers to his lips and whispered, "Wait…"

His brows drew together in a frown. "What? Anything. Tell me and you've got it."

"It's only…"

"Say it. It's okay. I can take it."

"It's Lola. Wes, she was hurt, really hurt, that you just vanished from her life that way. She cried so hard, she wore herself out. She just didn't understand how you could do that, go away like that. I explained to her the best I could that you and I were not going to be seeing each other anymore and that meant she wouldn't be seeing you, either."

His face had paled. "What happened then?"

"She finally settled down and went to bed. In the morning, she was better, but she misses you."

"I'm an ass. An absolute ass."

"Hey." She laughed through her tears. "Don't say mean things about the guy I love."

"Tell me she's all right, that what I did is fixable."

"Of course, it's fixable. With love and understanding, anything is possible. And I believe you, Wes. I think you do want to be with me, that you're over trying to pretend you're some good-time guy, some player."

"I am, Evy. I swear it to you."

"And I'm willing to try again, willing to put my trust in you. But if you break my little girl's heart a second time…"

"I won't. I swear to you, I won't." He peered at her more closely. "There's more, I can see it in your eyes. Say it. Whatever it is, I'll do whatever needs doing to make it happen."

"All right, then. It's simple. Before we start planning our future together, you need to talk to my daughter. She needs to know that you're back in her life to stay."

Chapter Twelve

Wes stood in the front room, staring blankly out the picture window as Evy's Subaru rolled by on the street and turned the corner on the way to the driveway at the side of the house.

She'd gone by herself to pick up Lola from daycare, leaving him to pace the floor of her dad's house and try to figure out the right thing to say to a little girl who'd cried a river over him just a few nights before. Lola's kitten sat on the sofa staring at him, as though she knew he'd messed up and he'd better get it right this time.

"I'll do my best," he promised aloud.

Valentina yawned hugely.

Faintly, he heard the garage door rumble up. By then, his heart had started bouncing around like it would beat its way out of the cage of his chest.

Was he having a heart attack? Sure felt that way.

The garage door went down. Not two minutes later, he heard the door into the laundry room fly open. "Weston!" Lola shouted.

"Right here!" He headed for the open double doors that led directly into the kitchen and family room and didn't even make it over the threshold before thirty pounds of little girl barreled into him.

"Weston!" She lifted her arms.

He swung her up and she wrapped herself around him, squeezing hard. She smelled of strawberry shampoo and chalk dust and he could have stood there forever while she clung to his neck, holding on really tight. "You came back," she whispered fervently. "I knew that you would."

Evy stood in the kitchen, watching them, tears shining in her eyes.

"Weston." Lola framed his face between her small hands and glared at him. "I don't want you to go away again. I want to see you every day—or at least, most days—and I want to go to the ranch and ride Babycakes and play with Archie."

"Yes," he said. "I won't go away again. I will see you all the time. At least most days. And you can ride Babycakes. As for Archie…" Where to even begin with that story? He had no clue.

Evy came to his rescue. "Lolly, Archie got hurt by a bear and he had to go to the animal hospital. But when he's feeling better, yes, you can play with him."

Still clutching Wes's neck in a stranglehold, Lola turned her head to ask her mom, "Can we go visit him at the hospital?"

"Not today."

"Tomorrow then. Please, Mommy?"

"We'll see."

"A bear!" She whipped her head around to Wes again and demanded, "Really?"

"Yes, but he's going to be okay."

She gave him a giant smile. "Good." She started squirming. "Now, put me down." He let her slide to the floor. She bent to pick up Valentina. After first burying her nose in the kitten's soft fur, she lifted her head and announced, "We should have grilled cheese and tomato soup for dinner to celebrate you coming back and not going away ever again for more than a little while no matter what."

He glanced up at Evy.

She shrugged. "Sure. Why not?"

A few minutes later, Owen and Dotty appeared. Dotty greeted him cheerfully.

Owen asked, "All good?"

"Getting there." He offered his hand and they shook.

The five of them sat down to soup and sandwiches. After the meal, Wes hung around. He didn't want to leave and nobody asked him to go. He got to help tuck Lola into bed and then he drove Evy to Doug's.

When he pulled into Doug's parking lot, Evy leaned across the console and commanded, "Go home. I mean it. You need some sleep."

"I might as well just stay in town. I want to check on Archie first thing tomorrow, anyway."

"You're dead on your feet."

"Yeah, well, I'll take a nap here in the truck."

She tugged on his ear. "You can't sleep in the parking lot."

He caught her hand and kissed her knuckles, one by one. "Whatever. I'll get a room."

She heaved a big sigh. Pulling her phone out, she punched in a call. "Dad?… Yes. Fine. Listen, Wes won't go home. Can you clear off that bed in the spare room?" Owen said something to which Evy replied, "Thanks. He'll be there in a few minutes." She gave Wes a look of great patience and then said into the phone, "I'm guessing he'll insist on picking me up after my shift."

"Damn straight, I will."

She actually rolled her eyes at that before saying

to her dad, "Make sure he gets at least a few hours of sleep… Yeah. Good. Love you, Dad." She put her phone away and shook a finger at him. "Sleep. I mean it. And call your parents, please."

"Evy. I'm a thirty-three-year-old man. I don't have to ask my parents if I can spend the night in town."

"Call them. Give them an update on Archie. Tell them everything is going to be okay."

"And that you love me and we're getting—"

"Shh." She pressed her fingers to his lips. "We haven't talked about that yet."

"But we will."

"Get some sleep. I mean it." And then she jumped out of the pickup without giving him a chance to steal another kiss—let alone to zip around the front of the truck and pull open her door for her.

She waved as she went inside. He sat there for a minute, missing her already, longing to follow her in, to sit at the bar nursing a beer until closing time, growling at any guy who got too close to her.

But then he yawned and that had him thinking that maybe she was right. A nap wouldn't hurt.

At the house on Union Street, Owen handed him a key. "If you're sneaking out of here in the middle of the night to give Everlee a ride home, lock the door when you go."

"Will do."

"Okay, then. This way…" Owen ushered him to the spare bedroom and left him alone.

Wes shut the door and glanced around at butter-yellow walls covered in framed movie posters. Stacks of stuff in boxes lined the walls and completely obscured the surface of an old desk. The two bookcases on one wall were filled with boxes, too—Owen's stash of memorabilia and old comic books, most likely.

Pulling out his phone, Wes sat on the single bed and called the ranch. His mother answered.

"Hey, Mom. Just checking in."

She talked his ear off for half an hour. When he could get a word in edgewise, he told her about the bear and that Archie would be fine and also that he was staying in town for tonight, at least. Of course, she had to know *where* he was staying and he said, "It's a long story, Mom."

"A happy story, I hope."

"Yeah, Mom. So happy."

"I'm glad. The past few days, you haven't seemed very happy."

"Well, I'm much better now."

"All right, then. That's what I needed to hear. By the way, your father says you left a fence stretcher, a roll of barbwire and a pair of fencing pliers out by the Ingersoll Breaks. He put them away for you."

"Let me guess—he fixed the fence, too."

"Yes, he did."

"That fence he fixed? It's where the bear got Archie."

"I figured as much."

"Thank Dad for me?"

"I will. As for your staying in town—is this about that pretty girl you've been seeing?"

"It is, yes."

"Bring her to dinner Sunday—and that adorable child of hers, too."

"I'm working on it."

His mother chuckled. "Work harder."

"I really botched things with her. But she's a keeper and she's willing to give me one more chance."

"Don't blow it, son."

"I won't, I promise."

A few minutes later, she finally let him off the phone. He shucked off his boots and fell back on the narrow bed, his eyes already drooping shut.

When he woke it was a little past two. He carried his boots to the front door, let himself out into the quiet night and locked the door behind him before pulling his boots back on.

The parking lot at Doug's was empty when he arrived. Evy came out of the bar just as he turned off his truck.

She came toward him smiling as he jumped out

and ran around to open her door for her. "Did you call your mom?"

"I did."

"Did you get some sleep?" she asked as he hoisted herself up into the seat.

"Yep."

At the house, he nosed the pickup in at the curb and shut off the engine. "What do you say we sneak around back? I feel a need to sit in the swing under that old oak tree."

Her green eyes shone extra bright through the darkness inside the cab. "It's late—but maybe just for a little while."

Two minutes later, he had her hand in his and they were at the back gate. He paused to close it quietly before leading her across the grass to the big tree and the old swing that waited just for them.

He held it steady while she sat down and then plunked himself into the spot beside her. With the toe of his boot, he set them to rocking gently back and forth. Hitching an arm around her, he pulled her in nice and snug against his side.

She leaned her head on his shoulder as they slowly swayed. Through the oak branches, he could just make out the sliver of silvery moon way up there in the star-scattered Montana sky.

Evy looked up, too. "Pretty night."

When she lowered her head and focused those

green eyes on him again, he said, "The view from here is downright spectacular." She swayed toward him. He gathered her closer and claimed her lips in a long, deep kiss.

"I love you, Evy," he said a few minutes later. "I never knew love could be so good. From now on, I'm not going anywhere. I'm sticking close by you."

"Oh, Wes, I love you, too. So much."

He cradled her angel's face between his palms. "Will you marry me, Everlee Roberts?"

She sucked in the sweetest little gasp at the question—but then, being Evy, she got down to business. "Yes, Weston Abernathy, I will—not now or next week, but sometime in the next year, if that works for you."

"Wait. Stop. Yes? You just said yes?"

"I did."

"Come here." He kissed her again, taking his time about it, savoring the sweet taste of her. When he finally let her mouth go, he guided a flyaway curl behind her ear. "Sometime within the next year, you said."

"That's right. It's once in a lifetime, saying I do. And I want a real wedding. I want my dad to walk me down the aisle. I want to have Lola as my flower girl."

"However you want it to be, Evy, I'm all for it, as long as it means you'll be my wife."

She searched his face and her voice got soft again. "I do believe in us. You've made me believe, Weston, and that is just one of so many reasons why I love you. But we need more time as a couple before we begin our married life. I need to know your family better and we have to figure out the ways to blend our lives together."

"Yes. I agree. Right now, though, Evy, I want you wearing my ring."

"Nothing would make me happier." She gave him a teasing smile. "Where is it?"

"I was thinking we could shop for it after breakfast."

Another trill of laughter escaped her. "Getting right on that, aren't we?"

"I want my ring on your finger for the world to see and that is a plain fact." He kissed her some more—short, tender kisses. He scattered them across her cheeks, on the tip of her nose, down the silky skin of her throat.

Finally, with another silvery laugh, she rested her head on his shoulder once more.

He cradled her close. "I've been thinking… You and Lola love the ranch. Would you come live with me there? Not right away, but after the wedding."

"Yes," she said. "I'd like that."

"I'm going to fix the upstairs for Lola and add a

wing for your dad, too, ready for him any time he decides he needs family close."

"He would love that," she whispered again. "*I* would love that. But right now…"

He studied her upturned face. "What?"

"We should go to bed." She took his hand and rose from the swing.

Together, they crossed the lawn and entered the house through the back door. She took off her shoes and he removed his boots. On tiptoe, they went down the hall to her room.

As soon as she shut the door, he reached for her. They fell across her bed together, kissing wildly as they tore off each other's clothes, both of them trying so hard to stay silent—and barely succeeding.

"I love you," he whispered when they were joined at last.

"And I love you." She gazed up at him, her dark hair spread out around her, cheeks flushed with arousal, her mouth swollen from kissing him.

"Always," he promised.

"Forever," she vowed.

Afterward, she clung to him. "Don't go."

He kissed her yet again. "I'll be right next door." Reluctantly, she released him.

He pulled on his jeans and stood by the door as he was leaving, the rest of his clothes wadded in one hand, his boots in the other. He realized at that moment that at last, his life had become what he'd once believed it might be. Eleven years of foolishness had finally led him to where he belonged.

"Good night," she whispered.

"Good night." Quietly, he slipped out into the hall. The spare room was only three steps away. Once safely inside with the door shut, he put his boots on the floor and tossed the wad of clothes onto the only chair. Still wearing his jeans, he stretched out as best he could in the cramped little bed.

Sleep took him down fast.

Lola woke him. "Weston!" she whisper-shouted at the door. "Time for your breakfast!"

He put on his shirt and went out to join the Roberts family at the kitchen table. Evy served him pancakes.

They shared their big news.

Lola crowed, "We're getting married! I'm so happy!" She jumped down from her booster seat to hug Wes and then her mother.

Owen was more dignified. "Congratulations. You're one lucky man."

"Yes, I am. Thank you, Owen."

After breakfast, they took Lola to visit Archie. The pup seemed better than yesterday. The veterinary nurse said that Dr. Sanchez would probably release him tomorrow or the day after.

Lola cooed over him, calling him a "very, very good boy," promising him that he would be "all well very soon."

A little later, once they'd dropped Lola off at daycare, Wes took Evy into Beaumont and Rossi's, the best jeweler in Bronco Heights, to choose her ring.

They'd barely walked in the door when she singled out an oval diamond on a rose gold band with more diamonds clustered to either side of that big sparkler in the middle. The matching wedding ring was curved and set with diamonds, too.

They drove out to the ranch to share their news with his mom and dad. His mother cried—from sheer happiness, she said. She got on the phone and called all his brothers. Every one of them—even grouchy Garrett—dropped what they were doing to stop by the main house. They congratulated Wes and welcomed Evy to the family.

Susanna and Callie came, too. They hugged Evy and gave her pointers on how to put up with an Abernathy man.

At ten o'clock that night, Doug's was jumping. The jukebox played nonstop, coins were lined up on the pool tables and everyone kept toasting the future newlyweds, Evy and Wes.

"Cheers to the Death Seat!" crowed a skinny cowboy in a giant white hat. "Finally bringing love and happiness instead of tragedy!"

"What are you jabbering about?" grunted the skinny cowpoke's beer-bellied buddy. "Evy never sat on that thing and neither did Weston."

"Yeah, but Evy was standing right there next to the stool when that rock came busting through the window, causing Weston to leap to her rescue. They got up close and personal and look at them now." A fresh wave of applause and whistling went up from the crowd. But the tall cowboy wasn't finished. "Now Evy's got a giant diamond on her finger. As for Weston Abernathy, he is hog tied and branded, tickled pink that his bachelor days are through. It's true love in bloom between those two and they have the haunted stool to thank for that."

The beer-bellied cowboy grumbled something.

But his friend only raised his beer high. "To love and the Death Seat!"

Cheers rang out.

"To the Death Seat!"

"The haunted stool!"

"To love in bloom!"

"Forever and ever!"

"Weston and Evy, amen!"

Evy laughed at their antics as she waited next

to the haunted stool while Doug filled her drink orders.

Wes moved in close.

She gazed up at him with a glowing smile. "What?"

"This." As everyone cheered, he gathered her close and kissed her sweet and slow and thoroughly.

Outside, a lone cowboy stood watching, his heavy heart lightened a little by the sight of the couple framed in the window and the loud cheers that accompanied their tender embrace.

They looked so damn happy. He doubted he would ever know love like that.

How could he? He wasn't a lover. Far from it. He lived on his own, worked hard, kept his head down and his thoughts to himself.

What exactly had possessed him on that night four weeks ago, he still wasn't sure. He never should have thrown that rock. He could have caused serious injury to that pretty waitress and he really wasn't out to hurt anybody.

It was the stool itself that got to him. From what he'd heard, Doug Moore was a good man, but Doug had made a joke of that stool. It wasn't right.

People ought to show some respect. They ought to stop joking around about that stool and remember the one who'd lost everything—including his life.

Remember.

But they didn't. They'd forgotten what really happened, how it had all gone down.

So yeah, remembering would be a start.

Remembering seemed to him the very least the good citizens of Bronco, Montana, could do.

* * * * *

*Look for the next book in the new
Harlequin Special Edition continuity
Montana Mavericks: Brothers & Broncos*

In the Ring with the Maverick
by Kathy Douglass

*On sale August 2022, wherever Harlequin books
and ebooks are sold.*

COMING NEXT MONTH FROM

(H) HARLEQUIN

SPECIAL EDITION

#2923 THE OTHER HOLLISTER MAN
Men of the West • by Stella Bagwell
Rancher Jack Hollister travels to Arizona to discover if the family on Three Rivers Ranch might possibly be a long-lost relation. He isn't looking for love—until he sees Vanessa Richardson.

#2924 IN THE RING WITH THE MAVERICK
Montana Mavericks: Brothers & Broncos • by Kathy Douglass
Two rodeo riders—cowboy Jack Burris and rodeo queen Audrey Hawkins—compete for the same prize all the while battling their feelings for each other. Sparks fly as they discover that the best prize is the love that grows between them.

#2925 LESSONS IN FATHERHOOD
Home to Oak Hollow • by Makenna Lee
When Nicholas Weller finds a baby in his art gallery, he's shocked to find out the baby is his. Emma Blake agrees to teach this confirmed bachelor how to be a father, but after the loss of her husband and child, can she learn to love again?

#2926 IT STARTED WITH A PUPPY
Furever Yours • by Christy Jeffries
Shy and unobtrusive Elise Mackenzie is finally living life under her own control, while charming and successful Harris Vega has never met a fixer-upper house he couldn't remodel. Elise is finally coming into her own but does Harris see her as just another project—or is there something more between them?

#2927 BE CAREFUL WHAT YOU WISH FOR
Lucky Stars • by Elizabeth Bevarly
When Chance wished for a million dollars as a teenager, he never expected it to come true—especially not via his late brother's twins, who are now his responsibility. Luckily, Poppy Digby has known the twins all their lives and agrees to stay—just for a few days!—but they each find themselves longing for more time...

#2928 EXPECTING HER EX'S BABY
Sutton's Place • by Shannon Stacey
Lane Thompson and Evie Sutton were married once and that didn't work out. But resisting each other hasn't worked out very well, either, and now they're having a baby. Can they make it work this time around? Or will old wounds once again tear them apart?

YOU CAN FIND MORE INFORMATION ON UPCOMING HARLEQUIN TITLES, FREE EXCERPTS AND MORE AT HARLEQUIN.COM.

HSECNM0622

SPECIAL EXCERPT FROM

HQN

*Welcome to Honey, Texas, where honey is big business
and a way of life. Tansy Hill is fierce when it comes to
protecting her family and their bees. When her biggest
rival, Dane Knudson, threatens her livelihood,
Tansy is ready for battle!*

Read on for a sneak preview of
The Sweetest Thing,
the first book in the Honey Hill trilogy,
by USA TODAY *bestselling author Sasha Summers.*

"He cannot be serious." Tansy stared at the front page of
the local *Hill Country Gazette* in horror. At the far too
flattering picture of Dane Knudson. And that smile. That
smug, "That's right, I'm superhot and I know it" smile that
set her teeth on edge. "What is he thinking?"

"He who?" Tansy's sister, Astrid, sat across the kitchen
table with Beeswax, their massive orange cat, occupying her
lap.

"Dane." Tansy wiggled the newspaper. "Who else?"

"What did he do now?" Aunt Camellia asked.

"This." Tansy shook the newspaper again. "'While
continuing to produce their award-winning clover honey,'"
she read, "'Viking Honey will be expanding operations and
combining their Viking ancestry and Texas heritage—'"

Aunt Camellia joined them at the table. "All the Viking
this and Viking that. That boy is pure Texan."

"The Viking thing is a marketing gimmick," Tansy
agreed.

"A smart one." Astrid winced at the glare Tansy shot her way. "What about this has you so worked up, Tansy?"

"I hadn't gotten there, yet." Tansy held up one finger as she continued, "'Combining their Viking ancestry and Texas heritage for a one-of-a-kind event venue and riverfront cabins ready for nature-loving guests by next fall.'"

All at once, the room froze. *Finally.* She watched as, one by one, they realized why this was a bad thing.

Two years of scorching heat and drought had left Honey Hill Farms' apiaries in a precarious position. Not just the bees—the family farm itself.

"It's almost as if he doesn't understand or…or care about the bees." Astrid looked sincerely crestfallen.

"He *doesn't* care about the bees." Tansy nodded. "If he did, this wouldn't be happening." She scanned the paper again—but not the photo. His smile only added insult to injury.

To Dane, life was a game and toying with people's emotions was all part of it. Over and over again, she'd invested time and energy and hours of hard work, and he'd just sort of winged it. *Always.* As far as Tansy knew, he'd never suffered any consequences for his lackluster efforts. No, the great Dane Knudson could charm his way through pretty much any situation. But what would he know about hard work or facing consequences when his family made a good portion of their income off a stolen Hill Honey recipe?

Get 4 FREE REWARDS!

We'll send you 2 FREE Books plus 2 FREE Mystery Gifts.

FREE Value Over **$20**

Both the **Harlequin® Special Edition** and **Harlequin® Heartwarming™** series feature compelling novels filled with stories of love and strength where the bonds of friendship, family and community unite.

YES! Please send me 2 FREE novels from the Harlequin Special Edition or Harlequin Heartwarming series and my 2 FREE gifts (gifts are worth about $10 retail). After receiving them, if I don't wish to receive any more books, I can return the shipping statement marked "cancel." If I don't cancel, I will receive 6 brand-new Harlequin Special Edition books every month and be billed just $4.99 each in the U.S or $5.74 each in Canada, a savings of at least 17% off the cover price or 4 brand-new Harlequin Heartwarming Larger-Print books every month and be billed just $5.74 each in the U.S. or $6.24 each in Canada, a savings of at least 21% off the cover price. It's quite a bargain! Shipping and handling is just 50¢ per book in the U.S. and $1.25 per book in Canada.* I understand that accepting the 2 free books and gifts places me under no obligation to buy anything. I can always return a shipment and cancel at any time. The free books and gifts are mine to keep no matter what I decide.

Choose one: ☐ **Harlequin Special Edition**
(235/335 HDN GNMP)
☐ **Harlequin Heartwarming Larger-Print**
(161/361 HDN GNPZ)

Name (please print)

Address   Apt. #

City   State/Province   Zip/Postal Code

Email: Please check this box ☐ if you would like to receive newsletters and promotional emails from Harlequin Enterprises ULC and its affiliates. You can unsubscribe anytime.

Mail to the Harlequin Reader Service:
IN U.S.A.: P.O. Box 1341, Buffalo, NY 14240-8531
IN CANADA: P.O. Box 603, Fort Erie, Ontario L2A 5X3

Want to try 2 free books from another series? Call 1-800-873-8635 or visit www.ReaderService.com.

---

*Terms and prices subject to change without notice. Prices do not include sales taxes, which will be charged (if applicable) based on your state or country of residence. Canadian residents will be charged applicable taxes. Offer not valid in Quebec. This offer is limited to one order per household. Books received may not be as shown. Not valid for current subscribers to the Harlequin Special Edition or Harlequin Heartwarming series. All orders subject to approval. Credit or debit balances in a customer's account(s) may be offset by any other outstanding balance owed by or to the customer. Please allow 4 to 6 weeks for delivery. Offer available while quantities last.

Your Privacy—Your information is being collected by Harlequin Enterprises ULC, operating as Harlequin Reader Service. For a complete summary of the information we collect, how we use this information and to whom it is disclosed, please visit our privacy notice located at corporate.harlequin.com/privacy-notice. From time to time we may also exchange your personal information with reputable third parties. If you wish to opt out of this sharing of your personal information, please visit readerservice.com/consumerchoice or call 1-800-873-8635. **Notice to California Residents**—Under California law, you have specific rights to control and access your data. For more information on these rights and how to exercise them, visit corporate.harlequin.com/california-privacy.

HSEHW22

When Chance Foley wished for a million dollars as a teenager, he never expected it to come true—especially not via his late brother's twins, who are now his responsibility. Luckily, Poppy Digby has known the twins all their lives and agrees to stay—just for a few days!—but they each find themselves longing for more time...

Read on for a sneak peek at
Be Careful What You Wish For,
the first book in New York Times *bestselling author Elizabeth Bevarly's new Lucky Stars miniseries!*

"Wait, what?" he interrupted again. "Logan worked for a tech firm?"

Although his brother had taught himself to code when he was still in middle school, and he'd been a good hacker of the dirty tricks variety when they were teenagers, Chance couldn't see him ever living the cubicle lifestyle for a steady paycheck.

"Yes," Poppy said. "And he developed a computer program several years ago that allowed companies to legally plunder and sell all kinds of personal information and online habits of anyone who used their websites. It goes without saying that it was worth a gold mine to corporate America. And corporate America paid your brother a gold mine for it."

Okay, that did actually sound like something Logan would have been able to do. Chance probably shouldn't be surprised that his brother would turn his gift for hacking into making a pile of money.

Poppy pulled another piece of paper from the collection in front of her. "I have another statement that's been prepared for your trust, Mr. Foley."

He started to correct Poppy's "Mr. Foley" again, but the other part of her statement sank in too quickly. "What do you mean my trust?"

"I mean your brother and sister-in-law have put funds into a trust for you, as well."

He didn't know what to say. So he said nothing, only gazed back at Poppy, confused as hell.

When he said nothing, she continued. "The children's trust will begin to gradually revert to them when they reach the age of twenty-two. That's when the funds in your trust will revert entirely to you."

Out of nowhere, a thought popped up in the back of Chance's brain, and he was reminded of something he hadn't thought about for a long time—a wish he'd made to a comet when he was fifteen years old. A wish, legend said, that should be coming true about now, since Endicott had been celebrating the "Welcome Back, Bob" comet festival for a few weeks. Something cool and unpleasant wedged into his throat at the memory.

He eyed Poppy warily. "H-how much money is in that trust?"

Her serious green eyes had never looked more serious. "A million dollars, Mr. Foley. Once the children have reached the age of twenty-two, that million dollars will be yours."

Don't miss
Be Careful What You Wish For *by Elizabeth Bevarly,*
available August 2022 wherever
Harlequin Special Edition books and ebooks are sold.

Harlequin.com

HARLEQUIN

Heartfelt or thrilling, passionate or uplifting—Harlequin is more than just happily-ever-after.

With twelve different series to choose from and new books available every month, you are sure to find stories that will move you, uplift you, inspire and delight you.